To Hull And Back

Short Story Anthology 2021

INTRODUCTION

Welcome to the seventh To Hull And Back short story anthology, crammed with tales of mirth and legend.

My competition 'reading, judging, procrastinating and having a mind-melting brain prolapse because the stories are all too good' trip was enjoyable this year, but it was as challenging an experience as ever. There were a multitude of brilliant stories entered, all exhibiting a variety of qualities that weren't better or worse than one another – just different. The shortlisted stories contained in this book are, in my humble opinion, the most imaginative of those tales, written with care, skill and a smattering of enchantment.

The anthology opens with the three winning stories of the 2021 competition. These are followed by the three highly commended tales from the runners-up, in alphabetical order (based on story title). After that, the other fourteen shortlisted stories appear, again, in alphabetical order.

A piece of creative writing authored by each of the judges closes the anthology. This is so future To Hull And Back competition entrants can see the types of stories the judges write and learn about their tastes. I hope this might give writers a better chance of penning a successful story for the next competition.

I'd like to express my utmost thanks to all the authors of the stories that appear in the 2021 anthology. It's an honour to be able to present them in this collection.

Chris Fielden

DEDICATION

Dedicated to the memory of Carrie Breeze and Julia Breck-Paterson, who both contributed stories to the first To Hull And Back anthology in 2014. The world has lost two wonderful women.

CONTENTS

JUDGE'S STORIES

ACKNOWLEDGEMENTS

Thank you to Alan MacGlas, Lynda Nash, Mark Rutterford and Mike Scott Thomson for helping me judge the competition. Alan and Mike are both previous To Hull And Back competition winners. Lynda works with me via my writing services (I'd also like to thank her for doing a proofread of this book). Mark and I belong to a writing group in Bristol called Stokes Croft Writers. You can learn more about SCW here: www.stokescroftwriters.com

Thanks to James Childs for designing the cover of this book. You can learn more about James here: www.jamesalexanderchilds.com

Thank you to Angela Googh for preparing the eBook version of this anthology for publication.

Thanks to David Fielden for building and maintaining my website. Without him, I'd never have created a platform that allowed the greatest writing prize in the known macrocosm to have been conceived and launched. You can learn more about Dave's website services at: www.bluetree.co.uk

And finally, a humongous thank you to everyone who entered the To Hull And Back contest this year. The continued high volume of entries has enabled me to increase the prize fund for the next competition for the seventh time. Without the support of all those who enter, this simply wouldn't be possible.

WINNING STORIES

EULOGY FOR A BASTARD

The winning story, by Emma Brankin

I am here today to say something tortured and trite. To ugly cry and make you all feel uncomfortable or perhaps I'll not cry enough and that will make you feel uncomfortable instead. I'm here to make a dead person sound like every other dead person. You know: *'beloved'*. I'll probably end up saying inane, obsequious things like 'I can never express the enormity of the hole

Stef leaves behind' or 'he was a kind, gentle spirit'. And I'll definitely say: 'He lived life to the full'. You know, before his body detonated unceremoniously at forty-two.

Yep. It's going to be a struggle to communicate who Stef was. To me. To others. All those many, many others.

I often find myself reading his last text to me.

'Can u pic up cat liter. i 4got.'

No x. Poor spelling. And I didn't even reply.

There was no dignified, profound, clean end. Just a red clot, tracing a path towards the off-switch in his brain.

Then: Bloop.

No gasp, no fight or fear. No chance to right wrongs. To erase incriminating photos. There was a person. Then. There was just a body. Functionless bones, muscle and skin laying on the cold tiles of our bathroom floor. His unwashed gym clothes next to him, his awful country music still playing from the speakers and his mobile phone just pinging away.

Once, Stef told me that when he was eleven and his mother was in hospital having her breasts gutted from her body, he snuck his first dirty magazine home. Said he panicked, didn't look at it, stashed it away. Then, the night she was finally allowed back home, he looked at her from the hallway as she was propped up in bed with a drained, grey face and he didn't go in. Instead, he went to his room and masturbated over and over to page after page of all those luscious, blubbery breasts.

He was crying when he told me about that. Naked in our bed, ashamed of his soft, pink penis. That was unusual. All of it. The crying, the limp dick, the emotional incontinence about troubling sexual episodes in his childhood. I was repulsed but... I didn't let on. I just stroked his back and listened to him weep for his dead mother and her scarred, hollow chest.

So. I've told that story today.

Not the story about how he volunteered at the Alzheimer's home for his Duke of Edinburgh Award and let that old soldier think he was his brother. Not the story about how he jumped into that filthy canal water to rescue the woman who'd fallen in. And absolutely not the story about him travelling through the night that Christmas Eve just so I didn't have to spend it alone.

When I found him naked on the bathroom floor, there was a moment – just a moment – when I looked away from his glassy eyes and twisted body. I watched the soap suds slip down the shower wall. I reached out my hand and squished them dry. I thought about nothing. Convinced myself the world was just me and a blank, wiped wall. Then, the paramedics covered him in that white sheet and he was swallowed up by the efficiency of death. I tidied up his clothes, turned off his music, changed the cat litter. Then I picked up his phone and read the messages.

You see, it turns out, death isn't neat. Death is messy and raw, it's a sheet ripped right off and a body cracked open. Death is stitches and gashes and slices. Death is time to find the problems, time to expose the insides.

So, I read about his endless betrayals, his embarrassingly unsatiated desire to be with others. I read how he'd refer to me as 'The Exhaustion' when discussing his affairs with his friends – yep, that's the men in the third row avoiding eye contact with me right now. I read every single painful, twisted word.

Stef really found fidelity *quite* the inconvenience.

When the ambulance crew were ready to take him away, I looked down at the pathetic shape of my partner, vacated and vulnerable, and, still, all I wanted was to keep him. For one final night, hold him in my bed, peel back the covering, split him open, crawl into his insides.

A few years ago, his old school friend got in contact, said he wanted a coffee. With me. Not Stef. This guy was sunken and ashamed as he talked and talked. Wanted me to know every detail of this holiday he and Stef had spent together in their twenties. They drove around Italy, permanently drunk and characteristically reckless. There were dares after dares. Nothing was off-limits. Screw that girl. Steal that horse. Do a runner from the most expensive restaurants.

Often the dare was to start a fight and laugh as their victim bolted in a panic. One night, Stef dared him to square up to this young boy who surprised them, who stood up for himself. Next thing, they were speeding off in the car as police sirens neared and an Italian boy lay very still on the ground, blood running from his nose.

"I see that boy's face when I sleep. Doesn't Stef?"

I paid for the coffees and left. I never asked.

So, I guess I was... what... complicit in his cuntiness? Wilfully faux-ignorant? Can I really stand here and condemn Stef – stamp my feet that my vagina wasn't enough for him? Because... he was bad. Bad to me. Probably bad to you. And you. And he was certainly fucking awful to you. And, I knew. Most of it. I enjoyed it. It was part of the reason I liked him, that I *loved* him. I was thrilled by him and his bad, careless, pig-headed behaviour. I was delighted to join in with his little escapades, his ego-trips, his disregard for anyone else's fortune. It was exhilarating to cling to his side as he took command of a room, for better or worse, as he picked his victim and unleashed his wrath. Just because. Because he could. It was brilliant. Until, it wasn't.

So, a bad person who did bad things has died. And still I stand in our shower and wish those soap suds were there, clinging to the wall. That was *his* sweat, *his* dirt, *his* filthy, sneaky, little particles of bacteria.

I think about him climbing into bed with me after spending the entire night fucking Carole Brightman after the office party.

By the way, Carole, hi, thanks for paying your respects.

I think about things like that all the time. And, still, I sit at night on our sofa sniffing his whisky bottle, listening to his terrible music, dragging a string along the ground for his stupid old cat. I carry on his donations to the breast cancer charity and I play over and over *The Shawshank Redemption*, waiting to hear his voice quote every line.

I have to remember both versions of him. Because, well, as this eulogy is evident, I am a bad person as well. But sharing this with you. Ruining whatever delusion of decency you had constructed about Stef the man; now Stef the corpse... this *has* to be the last bad thing I do.

~

Emma Brankin's Biography

Emma Brankin is a teacher from Glasgow, Scotland. She holds an MA in creative writing and education from Goldsmiths College, University of London. She was the winner of *Fugue Magazine's* 2021 Prose Contest and the runner-up in Writer Advice's 2021 Flash Fiction Contest. Other work has appeared in places such as *XRAY Literary Magazine, Reflex* and *Maudlin House*. You can catch her on Twitter posting about Tim Curry's acting career and her cat's daily movements via the handle @emmanya.

~

Emma Brankin – Winner's Interview

1. What is the most interesting thing that's ever happened to you?

I'm a drama teacher and tutor and I actually sometimes start off lessons by posing a similar question to my students and I'm only realising now how much pressure it instantly puts them under. I have no idea what to pick. Is it interesting that I once shared a plate of spaghetti bolognaise with Leonardo DiCaprio? I guess I'll go with that.

2. Who is the most inspirational person you've ever met and why?

Not Leonardo DiCaprio. Although he was fine. The day after I met my writing hero Joss Whedon in December 2016 was the day I began to take my own writing seriously. Being in his company really inspired me to take action. (I know Joss Whedon has become a somewhat controversial figure in the industry in recent years but I can't deny that his own writing and the words / advice he was kind enough to share with me has had the most impact on me finally pursuing the path that I had wanted to pursue for so long.)

3. Which authors do you most admire and why?

I adore the late, great Carrie Fisher's writing. It's so witty and off-hand yet somehow also directly to-the-bone.

I read a lot of Ottessa Moshfegh, George Saunders, Jenny Offill... My favourite book of all time is *Rebecca* by Daphne du Maurier so I have to include her.

Also, it's still highly possible that Louise Rennison's YA writing is the funniest writing I have ever come across.

4. When and why did you start writing short stories?

I only wrote my first short story maybe two years ago while on the Goldsmiths MA in creative writing and education. I had written the opening of what I thought would be a novel potentially, where a young woman was emailing then deleting the emails sent to her friends. I realised eventually that it worked completely as a standalone so developed it, sent it out to a few places and *XRAY Literary Magazine* were kind enough to publish it. I find short stories really challenging to write but I also like the compact nature of them. I like living in a character's world for, typically, a short period of time.

5. Where do your ideas and inspiration come from?

Anywhere and everywhere. I tend to think there's a story in everything I come across and then, when I try to write it, often realise I was wrong.

6. Where do you write?

I write mainly on my laptop and I like to pointlessly move around my home to find new places to sit and type. Somehow, I feel that doing this is a re-set and I can look at the words afresh.

7. How do you cope when your writing is rejected?

It's obviously not the outcome you want when you submit anything but it doesn't devastate me. I try to work really hard on enjoying the process and writing things that I genuinely like. That being said, I actually find the higher-tier rejections a little more frustrating, especially when it's from somewhere you'd especially love to be published in, because the close calls kind of sting that little bit more. But, you do have to have perspective and, firstly, a 'higher-tier' rejection is, in many ways, encouraging and, secondly, the innate arrogance of being a writer, of thinking your wonderful words, more so than the hundreds of other writers' submitted words are worthy of someone else reading, is kind of funny. Rejections help keep you reflecting on your writing and striving to improve.

8. Who has published your work before?

I was lucky enough to win *Fugue's* 2021 Short Story

Competition so I have a story called 'The Scandals of Christendom' out there. That's about a teenage girl's relationship with her imaginary friend Anne Boleyn. Some other places include *So To Speak* journal, *Reflex, Maudlin House* and *Flash Fiction Magazine*.

9. Why did you choose to enter the To Hull And Back competition?

I remember it was recommended by *SmokeLong Quarterly* and I'd just finished an amazing course with them, where this piece had started life as an exercise with Helen Rye. I just thought, *why not?* I didn't have any expectations. I wasn't even sure the piece truly counted as comedy as it's got quite dark, emotive moments in it... But I thought the premise of this woman saying the most dreadful things about the deceased at his own funeral was bleakly comic so maybe it had a chance of not being instantly dismissed. The whole 'driving on a motorbike to Hull' thing was pretty unique but also a little baffling. I went to Hull University and have fun memories of the city so I guess that also caught my eye.

10. What will you spend your prize money on?

I think I'll use it to justify the money I spent on the *SmokeLong Quarterly* course that generated the story. Those courses might be amazing but they aren't cheap.

In all seriousness, the winner's sum is extremely generous as are the runner-up financial rewards. It's amazing of Christopher to recognise that writing, especially if you're entering contests, can be an expensive pursuit. I'm certainly not writing to make money but it really does help so thank you to this contest for really supporting writers.

11. What has been your proudest writing moment so far?

I have to be honest and admit the validation and encouragement that comes from placing in competitions is amazing. It's nice to feel that you're not completely talentless. I was really proud to have made the shortlist of the Bridport Prize in 2021 with a story called 'Silent Retreat' – I was blown away that out of nearly 5,000 stories mine had somehow made it that far.

12. What advice would you give to novice writers?

Read and reflect on what you've read as often as possible. Ask yourself why the writer made those specific choices. But mainly, have fun and, ultimately, write the stories you want to read. That way, no matter what happens to them or how they are received, you should be proud of what you've created.

CATCH ME IF YOU CAT

The second place story, by Ian Tucker

A cat was lying on Colin's doorstep. It was black and lithe and designed for slinking through shadows. It was not looking at him. Colin put his key in the lock. The cat stretched and flexed its claws, squirmed onto its back and lolled.

Colin stopped the door from swinging wide enough for the cat to insinuate its way through and pondered his options. The cat spread itself scientifically to obstruct the fairway and pretended to be asleep. Colin tried to coerce it away, gently, with his toe, but the cat twisted and the exercise became like pushing soup. Colin tried to step over the cat and it immediately stopped pretending to be asleep and stood up in a way that made it a trip hazard. Colin glowered. The cat glanced at the thin space between door and jamb. The movement drew Colin's attention to a small tag on its leatherette collar.

Colin crouched to look at the collar. Perhaps, if its owner was local, he could pick it up and deliver it home.

The tag on the collar read, 'DO NOT FEED THIS CAT.'

Colin stood back up. This message shed a new light on the psychology of the owner, if not of the cat. He paused to decide what he thought of the instruction someone had felt entitled to send to their neighbours. On a whim he pulled out a pen and turned the cat's tag over.

'They're watching you,' he wrote. 'Flea while you can.'

He liked the pun. The cat didn't like its collar being written on and stalked off with an affronted air. Colin counted a double victory.

*

The following day, the cat was sitting on a wall with its legs tucked under it and eyes that looked closed but almost certainly weren't. Colin opened his door and turned to give the cat a smug look only to find it trotting towards him. There was something stuck to the tag on its collar. Colin squatted to see what it was and the cat sprinted past him, through the open door into his house.

He bribed the cat with some salmon in order to get it

to come near. It purred and rubbed its head against his arm as he tried to straighten the curl of paper sellotaped to the collar tab. The paper was covered in a rounded playful script.

'On next bus to Tilebury,' read the message. 'Send money.'

This seemed optimistic.

There was plenty of space beneath the words so Colin wrote, 'Safe house, 21 T'mas Broad, Tilebury. Password *Aleksandr Pusskin*. Ask for Olga.'

Colin gave the cat more salmon and, while it was distracted, propelled it out of the door.

*

The cat was sitting on Colin's doorstep again. It was looking glossier and fatter and licking its paws. Colin opened the door and the cat led the way to his fridge.

On the back of the paper stuck to the cat's collar was some different handwriting. Slanted and angular. It said, 'Beware, this cat is bugged.'

The cat was quite happy to sit on Colin's lap for the rest of the evening and watch *Tinker, Tailor, Soldier, Spy* with him. He stroked its fur and fed it broken biscuits, until the double meaning of a cat being *bugged* occurred to him. Then, he stopped stroking it. Very carefully he tore away the paper on the cat's collar and replaced it with a note saying, 'Message memorised and destroyed. Eat this note after reading. Don't feed it to the cat. We're not supposed to feed the cat. Perhaps it will turn into a gremlin.'

After writing this, he gave the cat a sardine.

It did not turn into a gremlin.

*

The next message was in the rounded curly script again. It read, 'Am back. Olga intercepted money you sent and tried to poison me with rare Amazonian frog. (Jealous of my femme fatale looks.)'

Rather dramatic.

Colin felt he needed to up his game.

He wrote his next message in code.

*

The reply came from the person with the angular writing. 'Femme Fatale is lying to you. Trust no one. Olga.'

Colin turned this note over to write his answer. He intended to be guileful. He'd watched enough films to know that the traitor is always the one who says 'trust no one'. On the back of the note was a string of random letters in Femme Fatale's curly script. It took him a while to use his own code to translate it. 'Who doesn't?' it said. That was, all things considered, a good response to his encoded question.

And he did like to consider all things.

After a lot of vacillation and changing his mind, he encoded another question. The cat wasn't feeling patient and he had to keep the doors closed until he had got his note just right. It was midnight before he managed to affix it to the collar and convince the cat, which had instantly changed its mind and decided to stay, to carry it away. This was probably one of the reasons why people use carrier pigeons rather than carrier cats.

*

At this point, the feline thriller's narrative arc was interrupted. The next message attached to the cat's collar was printed using a determined ballpoint and read, 'STOP WRITING ON MY CAT. AND DON'T FEED MY CAT. KG Burrows #21. MY CAT IS NOT FOR YOUR ENTERTAINMENT.'

The cat was enjoying napping on the new blanket Colin had laid for it on the sunniest bit of his sofa. Colin idly stroked its increasingly lustrous fur and pondered the possibilities. Might Olga be messing with his mind?

More importantly, had his coded message got through before KG Burrows intervened? He played with the cat a bit more before remembering that the cat was not for his entertainment. Then he gave it some cold chicken and carried on playing with it.

He released the cat back into circulation with only a short note saying, 'I have not written on this cat.' He regarded it as a holding response. He was still thinking.

*

The cat disappeared.

*

Days passed and Colin did not see the cat. He bought a fedora.

*

He passed by #21 a few times but the windows had lace curtains and nothing stirred within.

*

Colin found he was nervous and irritable at work and his backlog of export licence approvals was growing. He wondered how long it would take a cat to waste away if not regularly fed salmon, sardines, chicken and biscuits.

*

On Friday night Colin turned up the collar of his trench coat and walked to a cricket themed bar called The Third Man. He carried a newspaper rolled under one arm and wore tight, black, leather gloves.

The bar was not busy. A group had stayed too long after work and drunk themselves into a long night. A few couples were having intense conversations and a dotting of singletons looked like they were waiting for friends, or something interesting to happen.

Colin approached the bar and put a polished brogue on the foot rail.

"Good evening," said the lady in the red dress sitting cross legged on a stool. "Have you read *Onegin*?"

She pouted and used an accent that might have passed for Slavic if there was a lot of background noise. There wasn't much background noise.

Colin unbuttoned his coat slowly and leant on the bar.

"By Tolstoy?" he asked. He tried a gravelly whisper and was pleased with the result.

"By Aleksandr Pusskin," said the lady.

"Did you want a drink?" asked the bartender. "Or are you just here to pose?"

Colin and the lady in the red dress talked for a long time about cats, buses to Tilebury and the single red rose in her lapel by which he had recognised her. He said he worked in tradecraft for the government but couldn't tell her the details. She said she was ambidextrous and that her name was not Karla.

Neither could recall ever seeing anyone at #21. They wondered who Olga might be and laughed a lot until it was time to go home. Not Karla insisted that they leave separately and take different routes back to their street.

*

The cat still hadn't turned up. Colin printed out some notices and stuck them to local lampposts. They read: 'Have you seen a cat? Black. Wears an instruction not to feed. Likes salmon. May be a cipher mule. Or possibly a mole. Sleeper needs to know if cat has been compromised.'

*

Days passed and nothing happened. Colin looked at #21 on his way to and from work but never saw any movement. A few times he went for a walk and happened to pass #21 on purpose, but still saw nothing. However, the bins were put out and there were occasionally lights on.

One evening, having checked the street was empty, Colin looked in #21's bins. There was a single empty pack of cat food but no evidence of fish or chicken.

Colin was troubled by this and thought about it more than was really justified.

*

On his way to The Third Man two days later, Colin found a message on one of the cat notices. It was written in Olga's spiky script and read, 'Not Karla is double agent. The cat has seen too much. Beware honey trap.'

This didn't help Colin much. He didn't mention it to Not Karla in The Third Man. They were too busy discussing the possible need for a black bag operation to achieve a feline exfiltration. Ex-feline-tration?

Colin and Not Karla walked back together and Colin pointed out Olga's message on the cat notice. He watched Not Karla's reactions very closely but she gave no indication that her cover had been blown. She was more interested in what he thought about the honey trap.

It occurred to Colin that if she was cultivating false bona fides, she must be in deep cover.

*

The cat turned up again, sitting on Colin's doorstep without even the shred of an apology for its absence. Colin was so relieved he gave it double rations of salmon. He shouldn't really have done, although the cat seemed to have slimmed down a lot since he'd last seen it and it kept licking a sore on its leg.

The cat didn't hang around long after it had finished the salmon. It seemed nervous and eager to move on.

*

On his way to work the next day, Colin noticed that one of the windowpanes at #21 was broken and the glass was missing. On his way back he thought he saw a lithe dark shadow slinking around under the window.

18

The cat turned up an hour later looking slightly healthier. The sore on its leg was no worse. The only message on its collar was the original one which read, 'DO NOT FEED THIS CAT.' Colin gave it some cat food he had bought just in case, and watched it have a nap on the blanket. He let it out after midnight with some doubts in his mind.

*

Someone plugged the gap in the broken windowpane at #21 with a balled up tea towel.

The cat did not reappear. On bin day the bins at #21 were almost empty and Colin could not find any evidence of cat food, chicken or salmon.

He met with Not Karla at The Third Man and watched her use her left hand to sketch out some ideas in her bubbly script. He pondered the rights and wrongs of catnapping while she nipped to the toilet and he went to the bar for some stronger drinks.

On his return to the table, Colin found a note scribbled on a cardboard coaster in Olga's angular script. It read, 'What do you actually know about Not Karla? What do you actually know about the cat? Use newspaper rack for dead letter drop.'

Colin hid the coaster from Not Karla. Later when she went to buy drinks, he wrote a rapid reply on the coaster. He dropped it in the newspaper rack on the way out.

On the way home, Colin looked at one of the notices he'd stuck to a lamppost while Not Karla returned to the bar to collect a forgotten scarf. Colin was thinking hard and was in at least two minds.

*

Colin sat in his car in the dark. The air smelt strongly of the sardines in a box on the passenger seat. He was wearing black jeans, a black roll-neck, his gloves and a black cap pulled low over his sunglasses. He was watching the door of #21.

Not Karla, wearing an unmemorable raincoat, approached down the road. She stopped outside #21 and knocked. There was a pause during which Colin listened to his thundering heartbeat. #21's door opened.

Not Karla started talking to the person who had answered the door. Colin took the box and stepped out of the car. Wafts of fishy aroma pursued him onto the street. There was a movement beside Not Karla's ankles but it was slinky and lithe and hard to distinguish from the shadows.

There was a muffled shriek and some kerfuffle as Not Karla became entangled with KG Burrows. Colin was distracted by the change in weight distribution caused by the arrival of a black cat in a box of sardines and only just managed to avoid dropping it long enough to dump box, cat and remaining sardines in the passenger footwell and slam the car door.

Not Karla was gone. So was KG Burrows. The front door itself remained open. Colin swallowed hard and went inside #21.

*

The cat sat on Not Karla in the A&E waiting room.

Colin came back from parking his car and joined her. She told him that KG Burrows was stable but would need to stay on the ward for a while.

"Lucky we found them when we did," said Not Karla. "Too proud to ask for help."

*

The cat lapped milk out of a tray on Colin's kitchen floor while Colin made tea. Not Karla alternated between watching the cat, watching Colin and filling in a crossword using her right hand. She seemed intense.

"If *Pusskin* is staying with you, I demand the right to visit him daily, as co-guardian," said Not Karla.

"In case Olga tries to nab him?" asked Colin.

"Olga can't be trusted," said Not Karla.

Colin picked up the crossword and pointed to the angular script.

"Your right-handed handwriting looks just like Olga's," said Colin.

Not Karla / Olga fished a cardboard coaster from her pocket. It was the one on which Colin had written his reply to Olga's question – '*What do you actually know about Not Karla.*'

"Do you really like me as much as you wrote on the card?" she asked.

"Yes," said Colin.

~

Ian Tucker's Biography

Ian tries to find time to write around all the other commitments of being alive. Mostly mystery, horror and humour. He has appeared in the supporting line-up of a few To Hull And Backs in the past. He lives in Bristol with his wife, feral strawberries and no cherries after the blackbirds got them all.

TUESDAY

The third place story, by Marc Phillips

We review my goals. Jwanouskos reviews them. He's written them down. He's the goal keeper. He's perpetually pressed for time. I've quit trying to meld Jw into something I can pronounce. Should I laugh when people say what they say in the dailies? I'm thinking no is probably what he's looking for. They are his goals. Do I still see things? Yes, I see pretty much everything.

"We're going to step up the dosage of Seroquel, I think. Are you getting along with your roommate?" he asks me.

Umberto? Yes, Umberto. It doesn't appear as though we trouble one another.

The woman in the corner there with the beaded suede thing on, she looks like a luscious ceremonial drum, like she would softly go fwop in my ear if I thumped her flat belly. Are you allowed to talk to me?

Jwanouskos asks was I addressing him.

"Did I say that out loud?"

"Yes. You said something."

"Is she real?" Right over there.

"Melanie?"

"Are there more?"

I'm supposed to please go now. They're getting a volleyball game together in the courtyard. I'm supposed to think about joining them.

The self-involved brunette who won't eat and has a face like a gaunt horse because of it but would otherwise be very ugly anyway gives me the volleyball. A gap in judgment. The whitecoats are chasing Charles Binny again.

The mannurse says I assaulted another patient. Furthermore, that's unacceptable.

"I did not. I dinged Charles with the volleyball—"

Tiny Umberto leans on an ironwood cane, behind me. He adds, "You wouldn't have caught him."

"That is unacceptable," the mannurse says again.

"—right before you clipped him and bloodied him up on the concrete," I finish.

Did I understand that I was never to do that kind of thing again? Why, yes. I'd add that to the list.

Tuesday, my wife calls during the Monopoly game.

I'm playing opposite the plump pouter with the wrist bandages and the Mexican boy she is sexually active with. I don't even get to eat in the cafeteria since the dinging, but then these two haven't had their unacceptability exposed yet. Umberto never plays. He sits angry most of the time. I don't think they give him medicine besides the pills for his leg. The dog's move. It goes hat, thimble, dog. We lost track of which pewter figurine was the pouter, which the boy, and which was me. I only chose one of the three because there is no globen pewter Earth likeness with a flat spot in China where it won't roll off the board. I have no idea why they keep rolling the fucking dice.

An enormous white lady who smells like fried chicken says my wife called. Somebody healthy in the head can call you and you get the message and call them back, collect. I ask the big one can I have an Ativan. Jwanouskos said to give me up to four a day. I feel anxious, and I feel like she is morbidly obese and will die a long time before me.

"No. Maybe later."

But we'll all be different people by then. Things will have progressed, possibly beyond salvaging. Spun out of control, as it were. Aneurisms are insipid things. What if she has one? What then? She denies me the pill. I try hard to imagine her lying among buttercups, some angle less repulsive. I keep seeing Jersey cows licking her.

My wife says hello, after telling the operator she'll accept charges. Did I see the doctor? Yes, I saw the doctor. It's the same.

She ends with, "You don't have to live your life so hard, babe."

Really?

"Life can be interesting as just life. It is," she tells me.

Sleeping is the one divine thing we do, or the thing most envied by the divine. Turns out divinities can't sleep. He occupies us for a while, a renter, and sleeps. He leaves impressions behind in the mind bed. Some people recognise the outline and this drives them around the bend. They are convinced God is communicating with them, or worse, that they are divine themselves.

I bug God, but he sleeps in me as much as he did in Plutarch.

Umberto sits on his bed and listens.

Opinions abound here, like assertions that people need not be lunatic to want to end themselves. Though Umberto believes this, he would never try to convince anyone of it. He is not in the right place.

"I am not in the right place. Even if I was, this is illegal."

The lights are off because we don't control them.

"Tell me," I say. "Again." I hear him draw up to make his case. Several dozen times this week. He moans. He is the slightest person here. At sixty-two, by far the oldest.

"I was drunk when they brought me in. Whatever I signed don't count."

So far so good.

"That hearing last week? The judge says I'm a danger to myself. My doctor, my whole family took the stand against me. That felt like a street fight. He says, 'more evaluation.' And I'm here but I don't want to be."

Who does.

"But for drinking? That's illegal."

Good point.

Tuesday, Jwanouskos tells me I'm doing much better. He doesn't support this conclusion to my satisfaction. I'm on a pharmaceutical buffet, having one of everything, three of some, but I'll be going home soon. I will never be able to afford what I'm taking in here, but the State will help a little. I hear he tells Umberto that neither chronic alcoholism nor binge drinking meet the statutory requirements for involuntary hospitalisation. The staff's considered opinion. Though, Umberto, you will die if you keep drinking. This is fact.

The lights are off again. Umberto is clicking his dentures.

"I'm going home tomorrow."

"Where?"

"Crusas," he says, is home.

"That's good."

"Finally. I like you," he says. "You are the smartest one to ever talk to me. I'm getting a restraining order to keep my daughter away from my house."

I have no roommate since Umberto left. Business seems to have slacked off somewhat. There is a lull in admissions. Charles Binny is still here, but he is crazy way beyond interesting. I don't fill the hours I used to spend talking with Umberto. There is a week of hours twice every day now.

Tuesday, Jwanouskos tells me to pack my room. I'm on tomorrow morning's release schedule. Good luck.

"What?"

"Good luck."

"I thought you said something else."

"What?"

"I don't know. Anything but that."

He shakes my hand and smiles. We wish you the best. Remember the things we talked about.

It's a long bus ride over the mountains. Streaming

scenery should feel better than painted cinder blocks and the same black man slapping Clorox water on the linoleum in the morning. But feelings are restricted by the drugs. The thoughts wandering around in their absence are unclothed, like Charles Binny.

My wife is surely glad I'm back. The dog almost died of a centipede bite while I was gone. Sorry she didn't have time to clean the trailer better. It's been one hell of a day for me, much more than I'm accustomed to. I'm fatigued to unexplored depths, deeper than desire. The medication probably warns of this in a pamphlet somewhere. We used to have a house.

I am capable of tying a rock on a rope and twirling it at whistling speed and flinging it far into the high desert air. Fetching it and doing it again, in the other direction, until I knock out the phone line. I am unwilling to consider car payments, regular like an expectant tide, and collection letters that we collect that look like repetitious smudge art, elementary from a distance. My unwillingness does not trouble me.

Tuesday, a letter comes for me with a yellow sticker on it. The handwriting is shit or I'm not seeing so well right now. I ask my wife to open it. She reads:

Dear Sir,
You knew my father. His name was Umberto Garza.
My father died today. He was shot in the stomach at Bolin's Running Indian two days ago.
He asked me to ask you to write his epitaph. If you don't want to, that's fine. The funeral is for family only.
Sincerely,
Elizabeth Harns

My wife looks at the envelope and says it was forwarded from the hospital. It is a week old. More than that. They've probably already gotten the headstone, so I can ignore it if I want. I can't want to ignore it. I take the letter to the kitchen table with a pen and loose bitter war on The Meds to claim my grief but they have me surrounded on low, stable asphalt and they are apishly strong. I turn the letter over and smooth it out and write:

Let me be
Umberto Garza
date to date

Would she address an envelope and send it back to them? Yes, but you don't want to send that. True. I don't want to send it more than I have not wanted to do anything lately. Seditious want will lay me down alongside my friend. I know this. But send it.

~

Marc Phillips' Biography

This story is a radical departure from my first novel, *The Legend of Sander Grant* (Telegram, 2009ish), and my acclaimed short story, 'Pyjama Squid': (www.irishtimes.com/culture/books/donal-ryan-blown-away-by-winner-of-this-year-s-3-000-moth-short-story-prize-1.2344602). Sorry for the length of that link. You can also google 'Donal Ryan Marc Phillips'. My short story 'The Mountains of Mars' won the world's second largest prize for a single work of short fiction in 2005 (£10,000 www.fishpublishing.com/book/fish-anthology-2005/).

Over the past two decades, I've published short stories, poetry, articles/essays and a couple of non-fiction books. I was named a 'Notable Writer of the Year' in 2004 and some of my work is anthologised online, such as 'Different Than Any Day so Far' (www.carvezine.com/story/2007-winter-phillips), which was selected Editor's Choice by *Carve Magazine*. I've twice been nominated for a Pushcart Prize and *Best American Short Stories* anthologies. My foray into genre fiction ('Caye Caulker Tides') placed in the 2007 Crime Writers Association Knife Awards. I think that's the high points. It looks a bit narcissistic to me. I'm not that way. Anyhow, I'm currently at work on my next novel, *Tip Diebaeck's Corpus*, the origin story of a contemporary anti-hero. (188 words) (shit, now it's 192).

HIGHLY COMMENDED STORIES

HARD TO SWALLOW

Highly commended story, by Emma Melville

There wasn't much call for sword swallowing in the telemarketing division of the Lancashire Compensation Consultants.

Colin had tried when he first arrived – demonstrating his prowess in the canteen at lunchtimes with the knives. The main effect had been to put his colleagues off their lunches and had led to him eating alone. Eventually, the canteen had adopted plastic cutlery.

In no way did it attract the girls, though it was a conversation starter. Unfortunately, these conversations usually happened without Colin and contained strong warnings to new employees to stay away from 'that weirdo'.

Colin – who wasn't stupid, just a little romantically inept – was quite hurt, had stopped trying to make friends, and had consequently gained a reputation as a loner.

His mum was unsympathetic. "I'm not surprised," she said, "there's lots more interesting things you can do with swords. Some might attract girls. Why eat them?"

Colin had occasionally had visions of beheading his boss so couldn't argue with her on that score but didn't feel such acts were going to be any more useful in the office than swallowing them.

"Ask your Aunt Doris," his mum said. "Her advice on girls could be useful."

"I beg your pardon?" Colin gaped at her. "This is the same Aunt Doris who wouldn't speak to you for ten years because you married an accountant?"

"Well—"

"The sister you attacked with a frying pan when you discovered Uncle Steve had taught me sword swallowing?"

"Well—"

"The 'advice' you always tell me will be moonshine because it comes out of a crystal ball?"

"I've tried everything else," his mum snapped. "For God's sake, Colin, I'm getting on and I want grandchildren. We're not getting anywhere by conventional means. Crystal balls might be worth a try."

*

"You're nearly thirty and still living with your mother," Aunt Doris pointed out. "I don't need any crystal balls to tell me that's not helping."

Colin had managed to locate his aunt and uncle in Banbury via the circus' tour list on their website. His mum had come too but Doris had thrown her out of the caravan while she did a reading, on the basis that the crystal might be affected by negative thoughts.

"Right, clear your mind, Colin, stare into the crystal and let's see what the future holds," his aunt instructed.

Colin was fairly sure that the future held a long journey home where his mum decried everything his aunt had said, done and worn, in-between criticising his driving, but he did his best.

"I see a telephone," Aunt Doris said, waving her hands vaguely around the ball of glass in front of her.

"You don't say," Colin muttered under his breath.

"And a damsel in distress."

"Normally because I've rung them."

"And a sword. Romance is in the air."

"Oh, come on," Colin said, "that's hardly specific. Could you even put a timescale to it?"

"Monday," his aunt said, dropping the 'mystic' voice.

"What?"

"Monday," she repeated, "definitely Monday."

*

By Monday lunchtime, Colin had stopped assuming that some great accident would happen in the office. Nobody was engaging him in small talk – which was usual – and nobody had brought a sword into the office

– also usual – so he decided his mum was right about the predictions. She had given him the full scope of her opinion on the way home, and it had been a *very* long drive from Banbury.

Having finished a solitary lunch in the canteen, Colin went back to his desk and picked up his transcript to begin again.

He waited for the computer to dial several numbers and eventually somebody picked up.

"Hello," he said, trying to inject a cheerful optimism into the word, "I'm Colin, phoning on behalf of the public accident department of Lancashire Compensation Consultants. I believe someone at this address has recently had an accident.

"Shit," said a female voice on the other end of the line, "that's bloody good. It only happened ten minutes ago."

"Well, right." Colin stopped, that wasn't an answer that was on his script. "Er, what happened?"

"The armour fell on me, the sword smashed my arm, I'm waiting for the ambulance. Thought it might be them phoning."

"Er..." Colin consulted the script again. "We could help you with compensation."

"Really? I was moving the armour to the blue gallery and picked it up wrong. I don't really think I can claim anyone was at fault except me."

"Oh, OK, er..." Colin couldn't think of anything else to say so he settled for, "Sorry about that, perhaps I ought to leave you to wait for the ambulance."

"Just arriving," the female said. "Nice to chat but I've got to go." And she rang off.

Colin sat back on his chair. So, a damsel in distress... well, she didn't actually sound that distressed, but the idea was there. Seemed to be a sword and armour involved and he had spoken to her on the phone. His aunt was right and yet, so wrong. This was not a romantic future. He didn't even have a name.

Just a phone number.

Colin stopped in the act of picking his headset up again. If he went into the recordings that were made of every call, he would be able to get her number. You weren't supposed to, obviously, but he could phone to apologise or to see how she was.

Colin hesitated; he wouldn't even think of doing any such thing if it hadn't been for Aunt Doris, but if she was going to be right about things then the future needed a little bit of a helping hand.

Checking to see that no one was watching – which they weren't because it was Colin and nobody paid him any attention – Colin played back through the calls and wrote down the last number he had dialled on a corner of his notepad. He ripped it off and stuck it in his pocket. He could make a decision on whether he was brave enough to do anything with the number later.

Colin dithered about making the phone call all afternoon and then sat in his car in the carpark for another ten minutes at the end of the day before he decided that he would phone. At least if he tried when no one was watching – either colleagues or his mother – then he wouldn't have any awkward questions to answer except from the woman he was about to call.

The phone was answered on the second ring.

"Hello," Colin said tentatively, "this is Colin. I rang earlier about compensation."

"Blimey, you're persistent," the female voice on the other end of the line said.

"I just wondered if you were all right," Colin said.

"Apart from the broken arm, you mean."

"Er, yes." Colin felt this wasn't quite the chat up he had envisaged.

After a pause, the woman said, "Why did you phone?"

"Er, well, er, just to see how you were," Colin said.

"Well, that's nice. Kind of you, I suppose, but I am actually fine."

There was another awkward pause then Colin decided he might as well tell her the full truth; the conversation could hardly get any worse. "I'm sorry," he said, "it was just that my aunt looked in her crystal ball and she said I was going to meet someone today who was a damsel in distress who had had an accident with a sword. So I thought it might be you."

There was a slightly longer pause and then she said, "Have you met many other people today who have had sword related accidents?"

"Just you," Colin admitted.

"Did your aunt's crystal ball tell you what was going to happen next?"

"No."

"Oh good. I'm Natalie, by the way, and I don't think I've ever had a stranger conversation. What do you usually do with damsels in distress and swords?"

"I usually cause it," Colin said glumly, "by swallowing them."

The pause this time was so long that Colin decided she had probably hung up on him before she said, "Do you do that a lot?"

"Yes," Colin said honestly, "or, at least, I used to. Mum says it puts girls off so I stopped doing it."

"I can see how that might be," Natalie said. "Have you ever considered joining the circus? Probably more use for your talents than in a call centre."

"Mum would kill me."

"With a sword?" Natalie said, and then sighed. "Sorry, that was low. You are very kind to call and see how I am."

The pause this time allowed Colin to think that Natalie sounded very nice, that he was quite glad he'd phoned, but that he knew nothing about her; he didn't even know where she was as the computer's random number generator could have called anywhere in the country.

"There's a circus in the field over the back of ours this week," she said. "You've reminded me I was going to go see it one night. Maybe they have sword swallowers. I prefer trapeze artists myself."

"Banbury?" Colin suggested. Maybe his aunt's crystal ball was nudging things along.

"Oldham." OK, maybe it wasn't. On the other hand, Oldham was rather closer than Banbury.

"I could join you... tonight... at the circus, I mean."

Natalie laughed briefly. "I'll be the one with the broken arm," she said, and rang off.

Colin drove home in a slightly dazed state. Had he just made a date? Or not? Oldham was about fifteen minutes' drive so he could make it.

He sat in his car for a while longer when he arrived home and found, online, where the circus was located in Oldham. Then, without leaving the car, he phoned his mum.

"Sorry, Mum, I'm going out again, can't stop."

"I've made tea."

"I've got a date," Colin said adding 'sort of' to himself.

"Really?"

Colin decided he was out of range of whatever his mother might throw and he could always leave the call so he added, "Yes, looks like Aunt Doris might have been right."

He had reversed out of the drive and made it several hundred yards down the street when his mother appeared in the rear view mirror waving a rolling pin in the doorway.

*

Colin found the field where the circus had set up on his fourth attempt and then wandered round until he found a hotdog stall. He bought a hotdog and a bag of chips and then, for the sake of any other plan, went and loitered by the field entrance on the lookout for girls with broken arms. He had forty-five minutes to kill until the show started and nothing better to do. He tried to envisage what Natalie might look like from the sound of her voice but that didn't really help.

It was getting fairly dark, the show was imminent and Colin was deciding that he had been a total prat when he finally noticed a young woman hesitating in the entrance with an arm in a cast. She was about his own age, which was a start, and dressed in jeans, boots and a multi-coloured fleece.

He strode towards her. "Natalie?"

She turned her head to look at him. "Colin?"

"That's me."

"No sword," she said weakly, "wasn't sure how to recognise you."

"I could talk to you on the phone," Colin said, "if that would help." He mentally slapped himself as he realised he could probably have saved himself a long, cold wait if he'd tried calling her earlier. The one thing he did know about her was her phone number.

"You actually came."

"I thought joining random strangers with broken arms, halfway across the county might have more success than recent attempts at dates."

"Still following advice from crystal balls?" Natalie asked.

"I'm not knocking it so far," Colin said, "as it seems to be working. Shall we go and see the show?"

"As long as if they don't have sword swallowers, you demonstrate for me."

"I thought you preferred trapeze artists."

"Well you can do that too." Natalie smiled and Colin's heart proved that it could do some fairly interesting acrobatics of its own.

*

At the end of a thoroughly enjoyable evening where Colin had discovered that he was capable of chatting to a girl without her running away screaming, Colin offered Natalie his arm as they left the tent and she took it.

"Can I give you a lift home?"

"No, thanks," Natalie said, and then smiled at his sigh. "Not that it wouldn't be nice but I meant it when I said the circus was on the field at the back of ours." She pointed to the large stately home, which the circus was camped in the grounds of. "I live here."

"Oh, so when you said you were moving the armour to another gallery, you didn't mean in a museum."

"Nope, moving it to a public gallery. We don't need to look at it all day."

"Public?"

"Only way we can afford to live here still is to open to the public."

"Bit out of my league, though," Colin said sadly.

Natalie hit his arm. "Don't be a prat." She sounded alarmingly like his mother at that point but then smiled to take the sting from the words. "Come and meet Mum and Dad, you may be surprised."

"In a good way, I hope."

"Oh yes, Dad inherited the land but Mum's story might give you a little hope."

"Really?"

"Worked in a call centre for British Telecom. They met when she sold him internet. You'll have lots in common."

Natalie took his hand and led him towards the large mansion ahead. "And almost every wall has some sort of weapon on display that you could use to practise swallowing."

~

Emma Melville's Biography

Emma Melville lives and works in Warwickshire. She is a school teacher of students with special needs who writes in her spare time, concentrating mainly on crime and fantasy short stories, often inspired by her involvement with folk dance and song. She has published several poems and short stories in anthologies and won several literary competitions. Her first novel, recently published, was shortlisted by the Crime Writers Association for their Debut Dagger Award.

MAY CONTAIN NUTS

Highly commended story, by Karen Jones

In cubicle three, Lucy, who is built like a baby bird that's off its food, has just announced that, from tomorrow, she will switch from the fruitarian eating plan to become a breatharian.

In cubicle two, Iain – a bodybuilder who follows a time-restricted eating plan and low-carb diet – looks miffed. He likes to have the faddiest regime in the office. No food or drink except between the hours of 6pm and 8pm. Gym rota: legs morning, torso at what mere mortals think of as lunchtime, arms evening. Bed early, up early, boring everyone rigid about his fitness all day long. Lucy keeps upping the ante and it's getting to him.

In cubicle four, Rowena, who thinks of herself as willowy while others think of her as scrawny, picks up her 'Vegans are Sexy' mug and sips at her gluten-free clear soup. She has told Clare more than once that she is becoming increasingly Lucy-intolerant.

In cubicle one, Clare has just finished half a sausage roll she fished out of the bin – it was her sausage roll, she's not a monster – when she hears Lucy's announcement. She rolls her eyes to the ceiling then her shoulders toward her keyboard and stifles the snigger that tries to slip out through her sausage roll pastry-crumbed lips. She opens a packet of beef and onion crisps, holds them up in the air and shouts, "Anyone want some?"

The response comes in a wave of tuts and sighs and grumps and groans and she's-so-unhealthy-look-at-the-state-of-her comments from the narcissists she works with. Not just works with, but leads. They are, by quite some distance, the worst team she's had since she first started working at All You Can Drink Diet Shakes *may cause constant diarrhoea, thereby aiding weight loss* and Definitely Not Biscuits *may contain sugar, flour, butter and chocolate chips*.

Iain – very pernickety about that extra 'i' in his name – approaches Clare's cubicle. Even without looking, she knows it's him. His thighs are so big they push against each other as he walks in a swish-swoosh, swish-swoosh, swish-swoosh way that is slowly driving Clare insane. She looks up at him, licks the crisp dust off her fingers, smiles.

"What can I help you with, Ian?"

Iain glares at her. "It's Iain with two 'i's. You know that."

"Yes, and as we've discussed before, there is no way you can know if I'm saying it with one or two 'i's – that is, quite simply, impossible. Let's not have that argument again. What do you need?"

He nods his head towards Lucy, bends down and whispers. "She'll die. Breatharian isn't a thing. No one can exist on just air. I'm worried about her. I think you should talk to her."

Clare nods, takes a Tunnock's teacake from her desk drawer, unwraps it, bites the chocolate off the top and starts to lick out the filling.

Iain is transfixed. Each time her tongue digs deep into the creamy whiteness, his eyes widen. Sweat forms on his brow. Clare stops, puts her hand to her mouth in fake apology, shoves the half-excavated teacake at him.

"Oops. Sorry. Did you want some?"

He straightens his unfeasibly large shoulders and clenches his preposterous jaw. "Of course I don't. I don't eat crap and I don't eat at this time of day. I just need you to speak to Lucy. Can you do that for me? Please?"

Clare stuffs the biscuit base of the teacake into her mouth, chews, then sprays the words, "Sure, Ian," at him, covering his face in crumbs.

"Two 'i's," he mumbles, then swish-swooshes back to his cubicle.

Clare wonders if he managed to resist the urge to lick the crumbs, his tongue darting out like a loathsome, lying lizard. She's seen him at the vending machine plenty of times, and he's not buying water.

She takes a cheese dipper from her drawer, tears off the foil, and dips a breadstick into the gooey, vaguely cheesy substance in the pot. Before she can raise the laden stick to her mouth, she's startled by a Rowena-shaped scarecrow peering over the top of her cubicle. Gets her every time. Cheese drips onto the lapel of her jacket.

Rowena – very insistent on the first syllable of her name rhyming with 'row' as in a din and not 'row' as in 'row a boat' – always seems to materialise out of very, very thin air, leaving Clare clutching her throat and gasping for breath.

Rowena wrinkles her nose. "I wish you wouldn't do that every time I come to talk to you. It's not funny."

Clare looks up from under her fringe, Princess-Diana-style, pats a hand to her chest in fake remorse. "What can I do for you, Rowena?"

"You can not call me that, for a start. It's Rowena. I'm worried about Lucy. She eats so little as it is – have you seen how thin she is?" Rowena is talking to Clare but staring at the cheesy stick.

Clare feigns a shocked look. "No. Is she thin? Let me look." She stands up and looks to one side of Rowena, then the other. "I'm sorry, you'll have to move, I can't quite see her because you're so wide."

Rowena smiles. "Yes, yes. Hilarious, as always, Clare. But I'm thin because of gluten and lactose intolerance, which, somehow, you find amusing. She's thin because of these fad diets. First it was the Cambridge diet, then intermittent fasting, then Atkins, then that cabbage soup one that meant we had to keep all the windows open, even in the depths of winter, then the fruit, and now this silliness of not eating at all and believing she can live on fresh air and a little water. She's not a plant, for goodness sake. I do wish people would eat healthy, sensible food and not go in for all this nonsense. It's such a con."

Clare raises one eyebrow, whips the breadstick in Rowena's direction splattering her with cheese, and says, "Uh-huh. Uh-huh. And how many boxes of All You Can Drink Diet Shakes *may also cause constant tremors, thereby aiding weight loss* and Definitely Not Biscuits *may also contain eggs and vanilla extract* have you sold today, darlin'?"

Rowena trips her twig-legged way back to her cubicle, shouting, "Speak to her," over her chicken bone shoulder.

Clare knows a spindly finger will creep up and collect that cheese spatter and that it'll be licked clean before Rowena reaches her seat. She's smelt the cheese straws on her breath a dozen times. Frauds, the lot of them.

But they're right. She will have to speak to Lucy, not least because she's so useless at the job she could die in that cubicle and no one would notice because her sales target figures would remain unchanged. Though it's unlikely. Unless mini Toblerone is a fruit, Lucy wasn't a very successful fruitarian. A very sweet tooth, that little bird, so unless it rains chocolate raisins, she's not going to be any more successful at this 'diet' than any of the others she's claimed to follow.

At lunchtime the following day, Clare calls Lucy to speak to her in the staff kitchen. Lucy only comes as far as the door, seemingly now believing that, like a vampire must avoid sunlight, she must never be in the vicinity of a food preparation area lest she break the breatharian rules.

Clare has a tray of fruit on the table and next to it she has set up a chocolate fountain. The sweet smell has attracted Rowena and Iain. All three stand in the doorway. From a bag under the table, Clare takes a cheese board, a box of assorted crackers and a freshly baked, still warm baguette. The smells swim and soar in the air thanks to the fan Clare has placed on the counter behind her. The trio of dieters take tentative steps inside.

Clare smiles. "Right, glad you're here, Lucy. Rowena and Ian," she raises a hand to stop them complaining about pronunciations, "are worried about you and have come to me for assistance. I've been researching this whole breatharian thing, and I have a plan. What I think we should do, folks, is I should continue to do a lot of eating, but Lucy can come and breathe everything around me while I feast. Don't worry, Lucy, I've read that this is absolutely permissible. If you really want to, you could touch the food, but not eat it. You could even smell everything up close, but not be tempted to lick it. You know, so don't do anything like this." Clare stabs a skewered strawberry into the chocolate and then licks it clean.

Lucy tiny-tip-toe steps closer to the table. Iain's bulk casts a shadow over the bread. Rowena places a skeletal hand close to the cheese board.

"Apparently my sacrifice could be enough to keep Lucy alive. Well, for a few weeks at least. And I'm more than willing to put my waistline at risk to keep little Lucy living longer. But, you know, I can't survive on fruit and chocolate alone, so I'll also eat some of this cheese and fresh bread every day, to balance things out."

Rowena raises a straw-like arm.

"Yes, Rowena, did you want to ask something?"

"Will there be meat as well?"

Clare taps her chin with her finger, pondering. "Now that's a good idea. Maybe some roast chicken, smoked ham, sticky ribs — all those things that smell soooooo good. I'll see to that tomorrow. And this will be my diet for as long as Lucy lives. And no one else need know anything about what goes on in this kitchen. It's not cheating, but people are so quick to judge, so we'll just keep it between us, OK folks?" She takes another strawberry, sloshes it around in the chocolate, makes a slovenly attempt at shovelling into her month, leaving her lips and chin dripping with chocolate.

Lucy comes so close to Clare's face, she fears she might be in line for a big, licky kiss. Iain's fingers twitch near the bread knife. Rowena is stroking the brie.

Clare stands. "Oh, look at the state of me. I'll just nip to the loo and get cleaned up."

She stays away for ten minutes. When she returns, she finds the brie gone, a chunk of bread missing and the chocolate fountain much depleted. She pokes her head round the doorway into the office where her satisfied team are looking happier than she's ever seen them. "So, we're agreed then?" All three heads nod. A speck of chocolate remains on Lucy's flushed cheek.

Clare goes back to her own cubicle to sell health *see company's own definition* to the nation.

~

Karen Jones' Biography

Karen Jones is a flash and short story writer from Glasgow, Scotland. She has been long and/or shortlisted for the Commonwealth Short Story Prize, Bath Flash Fiction, Bath Short Story, To Hull And Back, TSS 400, HISSAC etc. and has won prizes with *Mslexia*, Flash 500, *Words with JAM*, InkTears, Ad Hoc Fiction, Retreat West and won first prize in the Cambridge Flash Fiction Prize 2021. Her work is published in numerous e-zines, magazines and anthologies. Her story 'Small Mercies' was nominated for Best Small Fictions, Best of the Net, a Pushcart Prize, and is included in *Best Small Fictions 2019* and the BIFFY50 2019. Her novella-in-flash *When It's Not Called Making Love* is published by Ad Hoc Fiction. She is the special features editor at *New Flash Fiction Review*.

THE QUEUE

Highly commended story, by Dan Purdue

Gustav hadn't intended to join the queue. He'd seen the line of people, of course, when he came into the plaza, but registered it with no more than passing curiosity. At that point, his attention was focused entirely on the wooden bench on the far side, the only one he could see that was both unoccupied and in the shade.

It was a hot day. Not just uncomfortably warm, as summer days in the city tended to be, but aggressively hot. The sun blazed relentlessly down from a cloudless sky, but its heat came at him from every angle. It seeped up from the pavement through the soles of his shoes. It radiated from the tall concrete buildings lining the walk from his office to the plaza. Gustav was a big man, used to breaking a sweat while his colleagues in the office still wore their jackets indoors, but this was something else. Parts of his body he hadn't thought ever came into contact were sliding over one another as he walked, slimy and sticky. His clothes clung to him: his shirt pasted to his back, the waistband of his underpants saturated. It didn't seem possible that one person could be responsible for so much sweat.

He was out of breath by the time he reached the bench, having broken into an awkward lumbering jog when it looked like a young couple were heading for it too. But they had stopped short of it, looked at a guidebook, then set off in a different direction.

Gustav sank onto the seat, let his head loll back, and waited for his breathing to return to normal. He pulled a handkerchief from his pocket and ran it over first his face and then through the thinning hair on top of his head. Then, he peeled off his suit jacket and lay it over the armrest of the bench. He took his greaseproof paper-wrapped sandwich and water bottle from his satchel. The water was unpleasantly tepid, but he drank most of it in one go, and then ate all of his sandwiches – apart from the crusts, which he broke up and threw to the pigeons that had gathered around him. With that, he gingerly leaned back against the bench, the damp material of his shirt now shockingly cold as it touched his skin. Then he closed his eyes.

*

He awoke with a start. The bottle had slipped from his hand and some water had splashed out onto his thigh. He opened his eyes. A man was standing over him, silhouetted against the bright sky. Embarrassment surged through Gustav, shame at being found like this, asleep and dishevelled in so public a place. He raised a hand to shield his eyes.

"I'm so sorry..." he began.

"Don't worry," said the man. "I saved your place."

Gustav heaved himself to his feet, collecting up his things as he went. The man was younger than he'd first thought − early twenties, perhaps? − tall and smartly dressed. In need of a haircut, Gustav noted, almost unconsciously, but otherwise very well turned out. As his thoughts caught up with him, he realised he hadn't quite understood what the young man had said.

"You saved...?"

"Your place," repeated the young man. He gestured to Gustav's left.

Gustav turned. Stretching away from him, all down one side of the plaza now, stood a line of people, their backs to him. It took him a while to comprehend what had happened, that in the time he had spent dozing on the bench, the queue he'd barely noticed earlier had more than doubled. In fact, as he found when he leaned out to look behind the young man, it now stretched beyond his place at the bench, with some twenty or so people lined up behind him.

"Oh, I wasn't..." Gustav began. But he couldn't take the sentence any further than that. He was surprised and somewhat touched by the young man's kindness in protecting what he had, mistakenly, taken to be Gustav's place in the queue. It felt wrong to reject this considerate act by admitting the truth. He also suspected that the young man had looked at him sprawled on the bench and jumped to the conclusion that he was too old and overweight to stand in line like everybody else. He bridled a little at that suggestion, and decided the best course of action would be to stand there for a short time, and then slip away, unnoticed and, therefore, unembarrassed. It could only be a matter of minutes, surely, before the queue began to move forward. That would give him the perfect opportunity.

"Thank you," Gustav said to the young man. "Much appreciated."

The young man just smiled back. Gustav turned around and began to wait.

By now there wasn't even a scrap of shade to be had anywhere in the plaza. The sun beat down, seemingly directly onto the top of his head. Still there was no sign of movement from the queue. Gustav felt sure he could not tolerate much more of this. But he could not bring himself to simply walk away.

He would give it a few more minutes, and then pretend he had received an important phone call. Then he would head straight back to the office and its wonderful air-conditioning. He wouldn't even have to give any of the people standing behind him a second glance. Yes, that's what he would do.

Gustav mopped his forehead with his handkerchief again and tried to remember whether he had ever learned how to make his mobile telephone ring by itself. If he didn't happen to receive a call soon, then he would have to pretend it was ringing silently. He was no actor, though. What if he overdid it? What if the young man or somebody else behind him caught a glimpse of the screen and it was obvious nobody was calling? He'd look a fool. It was bad enough being found napping on a public bench, but he didn't want anybody – not even strangers – thinking him a charlatan. No, he told himself, that wouldn't do at all. He needed a different plan.

He was so preoccupied with thinking of ways to extract himself from the situation that several minutes passed before it dawned on Gustav that he had no idea what it was that everyone was queueing for. He leaned out to one side again but could not see to the front. The line of people stretched all the way down one side of the plaza, only to disappear between two buildings, so whatever lay at the front remained unknown. He could, of course, simply turn around and ask the young man what was going on, but Gustav had now been there for at least fifteen minutes. What kind of madman stands in a queue without knowing what he is waiting for? No, there was no way he could ask anybody; he'd have to figure it out by himself.

As subtly as he could, Gustav examined the people around him. Looking ahead was the easiest option, although it only offered a view of the backs of people's heads. When he attempted to see the queue behind him, he found himself pretending to be stretching, or gazing at the buildings around the plaza like a tourist. The charade made him uncomfortable, but he was reassured by what he saw. Everyone in the queue seemed well dressed and good-tempered, despite the oppressive heat. The mood was calm, patient, and respectful. There was no crowding, no jostling for position. Everybody allowed everyone else plenty of space. He could see a few couples, and one or two groups of about three people, but most of the queuers were standing by themselves. Some of the men wore shorts, but there were no football shirts or garishly coloured sports vests. A few of the women he could see looked rather elegant in their wide-brimmed hats, large sunglasses, and flowing dresses. There was a range of ages, from the young man behind him to an old lady leaning hard on her walking cane a few metres ahead of him.

His observations of the queue yielded no clues whatsoever as to the purpose of the queue, but Gustav was pleased to be amongst this group of what appeared to be good, respectable people. He began to feel sure that whatever it was they were standing in line for, he would appreciate it too. It seemed unthinkable that this was the type of queue that might develop in front of a soup kitchen, or a clinic for some of the less socially acceptable ailments.

Taking one more look behind him, Gustav noticed a man standing about ten places back from him. The man didn't make eye contact, but was looking intently at him. He had straightened his hat and picked up the bag that had been resting on the flagstones beside him. Gustav realised with a start that this man was preparing to move. All Gustav's fidgeting, turning around in the queue, and looking about must have given this fellow the impression that he was about to abandon his place in the queue. Perhaps this man was simply readying himself and his luggage to take one pace forward as the line closed up behind Gustav, or maybe he had a more opportunistic scheme in mind – he might intend to claim more places than were rightfully his, should there be any confusion. Either way, Gustav did not like it. He planted his feet firmly, folded his arms, and stared resolutely ahead. He would not yield his place until *he* decided to do so. He would scupper the bag man's treacherous plans.

It was too hot to stand with one's arms folded for long, and moments later Gustav let them fall to his sides again. He sucked the last drops of water from his bottle and longed for a cooling breeze. He checked his watch, wondering why nobody from the office had attempted to contact him, given that he was now almost an hour late returning from his lunchbreak. Surely *somebody* would have noticed he was not at his desk. His boss, for example, who never missed anything. Or the pretty girl who sat opposite him. What was her name? Anna? Anya?

He quickly pushed the thought away. The last thing he wanted now was for his mobile telephone to ring. If asked, he had no explanation of what he was doing here. Such questioning would doubtless result in him admitting he did not belong in the queue. He took the device out of his pocket and switched it off.

It could only be a matter of minutes, surely, before the queue began to move forward. Then the mystery would be solved, and Gustav would end up with – at the very least – an amusing anecdote about how he'd accidentally joined a queue for... well, what? However hard he tried, he couldn't imagine what might convince so many apparently rational people to stand all afternoon in the hot sun.

He licked his lips, tasting only the sweat running down his face. Why wasn't some enterprising character making his or her way along the queue, selling drink cans from a cool box slung from one shoulder, the way he'd seen on holiday beaches? He closed his eyes and pictured such a can, cold in his hand, beaded with condensation. Imagined raising it to press it against his forehead. But he felt only the clammy pad of his palm, and smelt the sour whiff of his underarm.

Something changed. Gustav felt it before he had even opened his eyes, a shift in the mood of the people around him. There was tension, suddenly palpable in the air.

His immediate fear – that he had been discovered and was about to be ousted from the queue – was short-lived. Some fifteen or so places ahead of him, one of the couples standing in line had spotted another pair they knew and waved them over. They were too far away to hear what was being said, but the four of them were talking animatedly, laughing and hugging. To his horror, Gustav realised the first couple were inviting the second to join them in the queue.

Gustav frowned. He looked about and, sure enough, the faces of his fellow queue-members echoed the sense of outraged disbelief he felt bubbling up inside. What were those people playing at? That was *not* how queues worked. Everyone behind the first couple were effectively being pushed back – not one, but two spaces. It was insulting. The new arrivals had not earned their place, not like Gustav, the young man behind him, or even the devious man with his bag farther back. If the two couples wanted to stand together, they were free to do so – but at the *back* of the queue. He stared hard at them, the way everybody else was staring. Several people cleared their throats, rather pointedly.

It seemed to work. The two couples' raucous chatter and gesticulation became muted, and then petered out altogether. The second pair even seemed to be trying to make themselves look smaller, standing very still and bowing their heads a little. But those behind were not so easily satisfied. The throat-clearing intensified. People began to tut. The two who had pushed in looked around sheepishly, glancing away upon discovering they were the centre of attention. They whispered to each other.

They just needed a little more pressure. Gustav stared at them, harder than ever, determined to contribute to the wave of disapproval the rear section of the queue was directing towards the couple. The tuts and mutters escalated, and when somebody finally shouted out, "I say, there's a queue, you know," Gustav was only mildly surprised to find that it was he who had raised his voice.

The queue-jumpers bade a somewhat subdued goodbye to their friends, and walked briskly away across the plaza, not once looking back. Gustav breathed out for what felt like the first time in several minutes. A sense of elation washed over him. Justice had been done; the proper order of things re-established. He turned to the young man behind him, who nodded and returned his smile.

Gustav wiped his sleeve across his face. He stretched his arms out and leant his head from one side to the other. He wiggled his feet inside his shoes, bent a little at the knees and then stood up briefly on his tiptoes. He loosened his tie and took a deep breath. He was ready now. It could only be a matter of minutes, surely, before the queue began to move forward.

~

Dan Purdue's Biography

Dan Purdue lives and writes in Leamington Spa. His occasionally published, sporadically prize-winning fiction has appeared in print and online in the UK, Ireland, Canada and the United States. His stories have found their way into *The Fiction Desk*, a couple of To Hull And Back short story anthologies, *The New Writer*, *Jersey Devil Press, Every Day Fiction, Southword* and *The Guardian*.

His work has won prizes in a variety of competitions, including the HE Bates Short Story Award, the Seán Ó Faoláin Short Story Competition, the James White Award and Flash 500. His work has also featured in an English study guide, and been performed live at the Berko Speakeasy. One of his stories has been broadcast on hospital radio, although the fact that this has never happened since suggests the medicinal benefits of his fiction are, at best, negligible.

SHORTLISTED STORIES

BETWEEN WHORES AND GOD

Shortlisted story, by Tabitha Bast

It was Nora's fault, for she had left me in a speakeasy on 52nd Street whilst she finished her shopping. It was snowing outside, like New York at Christmas should be, but inside we all had misty auras from the cold turning warm, like corpses getting cosy in Hell. The woman who came over to me was not one who I would have approached.

"You want business?" she asks, straight up, and I catch the bartender's blue clam eyes and he just shrugs.

It's that kind of a dive, where the glasses are chipped and there's forgotten spots of dried blood on the floor of the urinals. The girl is not much of a girl now she's close up; she's 50 and hard-living, says the map of lines on her brown face. Yet another Mexican, and a voice as dry and unflinching as the whisky I'm drinking. She's as bold as the whisky too, the only one to approach, though this bar is rammed with pretty whores eyeing up this Englishman like wasps to a jam sandwich.

I could use a woman like this until Nora returns, keep those doll-faced temptations back. Would be too easy for a few minutes and a few dollars to enjoy one of the cute ones in the bin alley out back. And this trip to New York is all about healing my relationship from the last times that happened.

"Would you like a drink?" I begin, and the barman is pouring her one before she even responds. She laughs, loud as a warning siren; good. The bar is full of girls shrugging and looking instead to the door for the next load of money to stroll in. I silently nickname her Rentokil.

"You want full? Or mouth? I got a good mouth. Or butt?" She pats her ageing rump with her left hand, simultaneously swigging her rum and raising one questioning brow. Good multitasking, despite the fact it seems she's been in this bar a while.

"You missed the cheapest one. What about hands?" The barman glances like he doesn't know why I'm going there. I don't either, I want to ask him, he must have some wisdom on the matter, having seen it all before. His face isn't one you'd make small talk with though. So instead, I let him fill up my glass with this bourbon stuff that tastes nothing like the peaty scotch I really want.

"Not hands," she says firmly. "I have Holy Hands."

She lifts them up to my face. They are, for all intents and purposes, your average working-class brown hands. There is no light emanating from the fingertips, no face of Jesus imprinted on the palm.

"Holy Hands?" I repeat, not sure I've heard right. God is indeed moving in mysterious ways if here he is, popping in like an uninvited neighbour, here between this whore and me in this rundown bar. Though an alleyway in the rain would be even more uncommon.

"I will tell you the story?" she offers, with the 'will' a query like that Irish girl I had a week with, with freckles across her back like all the star-filled nights. Nora and I were on a break, so it wasn't technically cheating that time. Nonetheless, I didn't mention it; not all stories are for the telling.

"I was once a little girl," she begins, and I know it's going to be a long one. I'm a little intrigued now and there's something warm and beguiling about her. She suits Christmas in New York, and she suits this bar, and most of all it suits me to listen to her.

"I was once a little girl," she repeats. "And I swallowed fire on the streets of Mexico City after nightfall to bring the money home for my family. You may note," she rasps, "the petrol burns the voice box. I sound like I'm a smoker. One vice I don't have. But, hell, it should kill me even quicker."

I nod sympathetically. I'm a philanderer, but not an arsehole. Was a philanderer. Past tense.

"I had the same patch every day, and mostly us street traders looked after each other. And I was quite vulnerable when alone on the streets at night."

I nod and the barman takes it as a sign to top both our drinks up. "Yep, of course. You were just a little girl."

"Sure," she replies. "And… blind."

"You're blind?" She's looking clearly at me, rich chestnut eyes, nothing cloudy, just slightly bloodshot from the booze.

"Not anymore," she answers, triumphantly, and pulls from her cleavage a locket. She flicks it open. It's the Virgin Mary her Holy Self, with a big, red, throbbing heart.

"One night, I was working my patch when the streets were unusually quiet. There had been drug wars – there are always drug wars, right? – but it had been particular bad in our area that week and some women had gone missing. Older women, it wasn't dangerous for me. Not more dangerous than usual. You know anything of drug wars and Mexico, Mr Englishman?"

"Actually, I'm a journalist on a national paper, so yes, I'm fairly well informed. And I'm sorry, that sounds a difficult childhood." The brag about my status and my intelligence is softened with a kindness. I'm acutely aware that is my standard tactic for picking up women. I'm also acutely aware I'm in no hurry for Nora to come back. If I was an addict of sorts, maybe I'd have a band to flick at my wrist. Instead, I ask for some water to sit alongside the drink.

"I didn't make much money that night, the tourists were staying away too. I was packing up when I felt a blade at my belly, to the side, here." She grabs my hand and places it on her side. She feels soft and warm and that touch was unnecessary, which we both know. I linger a little, then pull away.

"Three boys. They all smelt of fish. And they spoke fast, like they were desperate, in high voices like they were kids, like me. And they sounded unsure, like this wasn't well practiced. But I was unsure too, and there was the knife, so I let them take my money. I heard them run off eastward, toward the docks. And after they'd gone, I was not scared of them anymore but scared of my parents, so I ran after them, following the echo of their boots and the strong odour of catfish. I was crying so much that even if I had vision, I would not have been able to see ahead of me."

The barman is pretending not to listen, but he's been drying those glasses for some time now. When a new customer tumbles in, stumbling drunk, I hear the burdened worker's audible sigh. My storyteller pauses, sips her drink, rolls it round her mouth like a woman in no hurry, like she's tying a cherry stalk. Two girls go straight for the drunk, one from the left and one from the right, and it looks like the scene before a catfight. He's a wise drunk though. He gets 'both the ladies' drinks.

"I ended up, of *course*, at the docks, where everyone, of *course*, smelt of fish. Too many spoke in high desperate voices. I had no chance of finding the thieves and my fear of a spanking wasn't strong enough to turn to, how do you say it, futile hope? I felt my way down onto the shore. With my pockets empty and my shoes on, I walked straight into the sea, clasping this very locket and praying urgently to the Holy Virgin.

"I would have walked on but someone took my hands and pulled me back to dry land. Beautiful, warm, solid human hands. And I know they were beautiful because as she steered me back to land, I could see. Her long fingers holding my short ones. Her Holy Hands blessing mine. She gave me vision."

"You're having me on?" I murmur, glancing at her hands. She seems sincere despite such a crazy tall tale. She's either a damn good liar or she believes it herself, because nothing about her is giving anything away. And I'm a good journalist, I can read a punter. And a woman.

"Holy Hands," she repeats, and we both look at the one on the bar then the one resting on her leg. The one on the bar moves forward and rests on mine, softly.

"So then what happened?" I ask. And with the question we get another round.

"She disappeared. My first vision, and then she was gone. I thought, at first, my eyesight had too, but no, that was still here. I could see the docks and the ships and the sea and the ports and all the people. It was overwhelming and fantastic and terrible all at once. I had to close my eyes again to grasp my bearings; navigating these so familiar streets was nearly impossible now I could suddenly see. I did what anyone would do, I headed to the nearest church to tell a priest.

"The priest was not known to me, the first church I came to was not my church. This was a mistake. But I was a child and, I thought, a man of God was a man of God. This priest, he sat me on his knee and he stroked my thigh and he told me to be good. He moved his hand up my thigh and he held me fast. But I was strong, I don't know, maybe I was still filled with the power of heavenly beings? I fought him off with my bare hands and I ran home with my eyes closed to find my mother.

"My parents were absolutely amazed. And delighted. My mother especially was a religious woman and filled with the status of my healing. She told all the barrio at any opportunity. Poor people love a miracle; it is free entertainment and free hope, right? It is our version of the American dream. Our house was soon full of well-wishers and gifts. Everyone knew I had been blind since birth, and it was obvious I could now see. My real priest was thrilled too – a place in the history books for him and his congregation. His church became packed. He reported right up to the top of the church this miracle that had happened on his little patch."

"It must have been like a big career break for him? And reassuring for his faith." My training has taught me to pull on the threads of a story, bring it out, take down the barriers. It comes naturally to me now. This is not the time for me to announce my atheism.

"So he thought. At first. After a couple of months, I was taken to speak to some men flown in from Rome. They interrogated me for several hours and I told them every truth, including about the priest who tried to assault me. By the time I was returned home, my own priest had denounced me and my parents demanded I confess I had lied or they would disown me."

"What?" I felt furious on behalf of this woman, not least because of the quarter bottle of whisky I'd drunk, not least because of the tears streaming down her lined face, from those definitely seeing eyes. "Because of that bastard child abusing priest?"

"Hell, no." She laughs again, a sadder laugh than before but loud as ever. "The church has plenty of those to deal with. Besides, he ended up in a ditch soon after, due to his righteous and vocal campaign against drug dealing. No. It was because of the miracle."

"I thought the Catholic Church liked miracles?"

"Ha, but the Virgin..." She strokes the locket. "She no gringo. I told them this, her hands were black, blacker than mine, her face, her hair is afro. I would tell everyone who came to me for blessing that those blue eyes were a lie. So the people stopped coming and the church kept my story quiet. Instead of being a saint, I started turning tricks with another fire-eater. And here I am. But I love the Virgin, and I won't touch men with my Holy Hands."

We had finished the story and we'd finished our drinks. My head felt a little dizzy from both. I reached into my wallet for the stash I was carrying with me like a tourist who knew he could always win a brawl. I paid the bartender a generous tip, despite his continued sullen demeanour. And just as he tipped some change into my hand, Nora appeared in the doorway, wheezing like she'd run, with hands full of excess bags and pointless purchases. Her nose and cheeks were pink, and her makeup had run. I wanted – immediately – to take her to bed. I told her we'd pick up a bottle on the way back to the hotel, and I waved a wistful goodbye to my new friend. She waved back with her Holy Hands. Nora stiffened, then ran a quick, critical eye over her, and relaxed.

We were naked, hours later, exhausted and so in love, both lying in a wet patch because there was more than one. I was drunker and she was drunk. I nearly asked her to marry me, but instead said, "Room service? Forget going out, I want more of this…" I ran my hands over her smooth, strong body.

It was only when the boy turned up with sandwiches and champagne that I realised my well-stuffed wallet was now gone. Presumed stolen by her sacred fingers. I had no choice but to tell Nora everything, from my temptation by the girls at the bar to the miracle itself. She sat in stony and clothed silence throughout my whole pitiful explanation.

"You can't be angry. Don't you DARE be angry," I rage at her. "I didn't even touch with anyone. I stayed utterly faithful in a bar full of women and drink and with you gone – shopping – for hours." She pulled her dressing gown tighter around her, nibbled piously at a sandwich, then placed it back on the tray. I watched her long fingers in silent fury, and imagined they were instead those thieving Holy Hands.

~

Tabitha Bast's Biography

Tabitha Bast lives with a child and a cat in a cooperative community in inner-city Leeds, and works as a sex and relationship therapist. Writings range from political articles to fictional short stories.

Previous work included in *Eclectica Magazine*, *Plan C* and *Novara Media* online, and in print in *Shift*, *Dysophia*, and a chapter in a book *Occupy Everything*. Won first prize with Grist publisher anthology *Protest*, runner up with Creative Futures. Most recently have had short story 'There is Life at This Level' published this year with Parracombe Prize, and an article 'The Boys are Alright' with *Dope Magazine*.

DA

Shortlisted story, by John Holland

Mrs Doherty said Da's head hadn't so much rolled down Clare Road as bounced. That mothers walking to school had pulled their children to their stomachs shading them with their winter coats from The Terrible Sight.

Mrs Doherty said that Da wasn't the kind who would have wanted A Lingering Death.

"He was an impatient man," she said. "At least he always was with me." I wanted to ask her what she meant but couldn't.

"It would have been quick," she said. "That's nice for him. But not for you — the family."

I can think of things Da would have found nicer than being decapitated at 10am on a Tuesday morning on the Clare Road. A drink with his mates at Gogarthy's, for instance — and home happy and drunk. Collecting his winnings from Declan Cullen's betting shop — and home happy and drunk. A trip to his beloved public library. Returning with three or four new books, although he may have left the place with six. Lending them to strangers on the way home. Or dropping them. And home happy and drunk.

When it came out, the brakes on his thirty-year-old Chevette had failed. He'd been driving down the hill, on his way to look in the fields around Kennedy Bend where Ma had said she'd seen an angel last week. Bobby Lynch's reclamation lorry, in front of him, stopped at the lights, but Da's car, fuelled by Murco and gravity, tore its way beneath the lorry. Or at least most of his car did. The upper part, the part that included his head, hit the back of the lorry, and came off.

"Poor Bobby Lynch, God-love-him," Mrs Doherty said. "Sitting at the lights. There's a crash behind him, and even before he's out of his cab, he sees your da's head bobbling by, gathering pace, ignoring the red light, and bouncing clean over Eamonn Dougan's battered Land Rover and into the Fill Me Up, Darlin' service station. Where it hit a wall before falling under the wheels of the reversing Murco petrol wagon.

"He was dead by then, Marie," she added.

"You don't say. What are you — the feckin' coroner?" I said.

"I'm sorry, Marie," she said, as if she wasn't. "But at least he didn't drive into the river."

"Of course," I said, although I thought the irony lost on Mrs Doherty.

*

Ma said that he couldn't make his Entrance into Heaven looking like that.

"Or even the Other Place."

She insisted on laying him out in his coffin in the parlour before the funeral. This put Some Pressure on Smiling Mr Carty of Carty's Funeral Parlour. But he was A Man Up To The Job.

"The human head is like a football," he explained. "We put duct tape over your late father's mouth and one nostril, then use a tube in his other nostril and a foot pump – you know, the type you use for pumping up a football or a li-lo – to force in the air. His poor squashed head will inflate. Of course some residual air will be emitted from his ears, and, in your father's case, from his open neck."

The results were extraordinary. Granted, laid out in Mr Carty's Trinity solid oak coffin, with the head of Mary carved into the side panels, with brass clasps and handles, his head and body swathed in white satin, dressed in his Sunday blue suit from Ryan's the Tailors, he didn't look like Da, but he did look like he'd once been human. Almost human anyway.

And although he now had the widest smile, and indeed the widest moustache, you ever saw – ear to ear they were – Ma was impressed.

"It's taken years off him," she said.

His brother Ronnie was more pointed. "Like a child has painted a face on a feckin' balloon."

It wasn't easy to lean into the coffin to kiss him. He

was cold, as I imagined he would be, and after, when I looked in the mirror, it was as if I had been having an affair with Boy George. Or was Boy George. There was so much of Da's make-up on my face. And so much less on his. I carefully re-painted him with my Revlon. To Be Fair to Smiling Mr Carty he came round each of the three days that Da was in the parlour to touch him up.

He had also dressed Da in a brand new high collared white shirt to hide what he described as the Rather Heavy Stitching used to re-attach his head.

Ronnie's children, JohnJo, JoJo and Ken, my cousins – feckless young men all – were, like their father, less complimentary about Da's appearance. "The face of a bloated clown and the body of Harry Hill," one of them said.

It was after their second visit, when they left the house sniggering behind their hands, that I noticed a line of five ball point pens in Da's top pocket. I left them there. Da would have seen the joke. Grinned his broad moustachioed grin, and rubbed his comfortable cardigan stomach.

*

When Ma woke from her afternoon sleep she called out, "What's that noise? Is it heavy breathing? Do you have a man in your room, Marie? Again?"

"Mr Carty says Da's head is deflating so he's re-pumping it," I told her.

"Is this a dream?" she asked.

Standing in the parlour, covered in perspiration from the pumping, Smiling Mr Carty explained to us how the formaldehyde was preserving Da.

Uncle Ronnie said we should insert Da in the fish

tank, claim he was an installation by Damien Hirst, and put him up for auction.

*

By Day Three there was a gathering smell in the parlour, and Ma stopped walking the streets inviting people to Pay Their Respects. When The Smell got worse Ma said it might be a Big Cheese she had in the Cupboard. I didn't believe A Word Of It, especially when I walked in the parlour and saw Mr Carty waving a bottle of Charlie over the casket.

*

Before the funeral, Ma asked us – the close family – if we wanted anything of Da's as a keepsake. I requested his copy of Flann O'Brien's *At Swim-Two-Birds*, yellowed and dilapidated through reading and re-reading – the lovely grubby hand of my father upon it. Nan asked for his black-rimmed specs. And Uncle Ronnie for his weekly bar spend at Gogarthy's.

*

When we arrived at the funeral, there was already a crowd. We parked the car next to the hearse – in the shadow of the monolith of St Peters. The dark lopsided stones of the church graveyard looked like big versions of Nan's teeth. But the day itself was brash blue. I could feel everyone's eyes on us, measuring our grief, but when I looked back they turned away. It seemed that the whole town was there, dressed in black or navy, having skipped lunch in the hope of an invitation to the wake at the Silver Shamrock Hotel.

I had to take Nan's arm and lead her towards the church. She was wearing Da's black-rimmed specs and looked like a tiny wizened Michael Caine. "Not a lot of people know this, Marie," she said. "But I can't see A Blind Thing."

The pallbearers heaved the coffin from the hearse and hoisted it on their shoulders. Had we chosen with more care we'd have had Six Big Men. Five were Up To The Job, but the Sixth was Declan Cullen from the betting shop. Less than five feet tall, God-love-him, his trouser bottoms flapping over his shoes and his suit jacket near down to his knees, he was lifted clean off the ground with the casket, and hung by his finger tips from one corner, legs flailing, like a monkey dangling from a baobab tree.

It was either a stiffener before he left the bar, or the combined weight of Da and Declan, that made Gogarthy's Cillian Clooney, sweating like a heavy-weight boxer, stumble on the rough ground outside the church. The casket lurched downwards. Horror and panic distorted the men's faces. But little Declan came into his own. His feet briefly on the ground, he stood his tallest, his arms raised above his head, pushing the casket skywards until Cillian regained his footing and his grasp on the box.

A Funeral Incident was averted.

But after that, a Loud Rolling Sound came with every movement of the casket. It seemed to run the full length of the box. Then back again. And so on. We all knew what it was. Some of the watchers took out handkerchiefs. Others hid their laughter behind their hands. Mr Carty, his normally crescent mouth now like a pastry crust, looked horrified.

Ronnie said that Da always enjoyed a game of pinball.

As we entered the church, Ma whispered to Smiling Mr Carty about opening the coffin and re-attaching Da's head.

Smiling Mr Carty said he didn't think that would be practical. "And anyway," he said. "He will be a Whole Person in heaven."

"What makes you so sure?" said Ma.

"Have you ever seen an angel without a head?" he said.

"No," she replied. "But I have seen a huge bird made from metal fly across the heavens."

"That'll be an aeroplane," said Smiling Mr Carty, patting her arm in the sure knowledge that our entire family was mad.

~

John Holland's Biography

John Holland is a short fiction author from Gloucestershire in the UK. He started writing aged fifty-nine and, ten years on, has won first prize in short fiction competitions on five occasions, including To Hull And Back in 2018.

His work, which is often darkly comic, has been published more than a hundred times in print anthologies and online, including in *The Molotov Cocktail, Truffle Magazine, The Phare, Spelk, Ellipsis Zine, The Cabinet of Heed, Reflex Fiction, Storgy, Riot Act* and *NFFD*. John also runs the twice-yearly event Stroud Short Stories.

Website: www.johnhollandwrites.com

Twitter: @JohnHol88897218

DEFLATED MERMAIDS

Shortlisted story, by Lauren Guyatt

The box he brought her in was invasive and felt permanent even before entering our tiny mobile abode. He wrestled with the screen door that refused to cooperate unless his foot was there to prop it open and, with his recently deceased mother no longer around to jump up and come to his aid, he struggled while I watched from the living room. His mother always liked having to help people get inside but was never welcoming once they were comfortable.

This boxed gift he had supposedly ordered for me was actually for him, which was typical of his demeanour. A lotto ticket, a pack of smokes and this summer's latest addition, the above ground pool. I can't swim, let alone drink, gamble or smoke while trying to stay afloat.

"Susie Q, this is Claudia," he announced hesitantly as he sat her down on the couch next to me, where I was propped up like a plank of wood. I could feel his mother's disappointed spirit in the room.

He wormed his way in-between us and started reading Claudia's lengthy manual while rubbing her thigh. There weren't any complicated instructions for myself when I arrived years ago. Written on the side of the box I came folded up in was nothing but a simple warning, 'Blow up doll is not a floatation device', which he had ignored several times.

I was your standard model: short blonde painted on hair, open round mouth with bright red lipstick only a man would choose, blue eye shadow only a hooker would choose, and hands that looked like flesh mittens. A mouth hole, front hole and a back one for special occasions.

My least attractive quality would have to be my pointy sharp tits. My nipples were where the plastic seams met, and you could easily slice your finger on them. My second least attractive quality would be my dislike for change.

Claudia, on the other hand, was made from silicone and looked like a real unattainable woman, complete with a firm round ass and generous bosom. Her face was stretched over a robotic frame. I could see some of the metal revealing itself just above where the lower eyelashes met the iris. The manufacturers must have missed it having never actually looked at her eyes.

I was more flexible than she was, with her bulky silicone body, but I bent at a sharp ninety-degree angle where as she could be moved into these graceful ballerina-esque poses like the one that twirled in my jewellery box as a child.

She made three facial expressions, all of which were too cheerful for my liking. She was also capable of a real fake orgasm and with that I knew I was in trouble.

"Wow, it says she can even remember my birthday," he squealed.

Excuse me? I thought. Did he forget that I always got him a cake and used my other hand on his birthday, which I remembered without an advanced robot sized brain.

She was the very first robot model. They were currently on number XF576, the XF standing for extreme fornication, which meant the price per unit had reduced significantly as newer models came out, similar to an iPhone. This is how my boss was finally able to afford her on his scratch ticket budget.

Her first night at our place, I decided to package her back up after removing her legs and put her outside, hoping those porch thieves the news was always reporting on would take her away. I wanted to ring a dinner bell and softly call out, "Come and get her," but I think that only works for cartoon dogs and wolves, depending on the setting. I watched a lot of television, which has helped me learn but has also left me slightly dramatic.

If not the scavengers, maybe it would at least rain and she'd short-circuit or something. Catch fire? I'm not sure how that works being full of hot air myself. He would always tell me that I was the sexiest airhead he had ever dated and laughed while I wondered how many there were before me.

He laboured trying to figure out how to turn her on. He had read the manual cover to cover, which showed his dedication to this harlot and how slow of a reader he was.

You had to turn her on sexually in order to turn her on manually and it took him too long to figure this out as foreplay wasn't within his range of sexual knowledge and he was forced to resort back to screwing me while he stared at her for the first couple of days.

I told him, a couple of compliments, some circles around the nipples, as well as a few lower ones, would get her there. I don't know why I did. I didn't want to lose him to her.

After a week, we discovered that she could talk. We were at a drive-thru when the voice box asked if we wanted to increase our fry size to which she responded, "You're a big growing boy."

The woman on the other end fell silent then asked us to proceed to the second window. We all giggled our way there then tried to hold it in as she handed us our fried food and sodas.

"I don't know why you're so upset," he said over a midnight snack of saltines and a brick of marble cheese while Claudia slept. "You know I bought her to keep you company, you're always complaining about how bored you are around the house by yourself all day. That's why I got such an ugly brown haired woman, so you wouldn't feel bad."

None of this made me feel good.

As soon as he left that morning, I had her get to work. I made her lick his boots clean on her tramp knees, with her tramp tongue. Same with the kitchen floor and toilet. Tramp knees, tramp tongue.

When he got home he told us how great the place looked. I said thank you and she remained silent, as I had instructed.

After dinner and his eighth beer, we all sat out back around the fire. He lit a cigarette, which always made me think about the lungs of a smoker they displayed on those posters in the doctor's office. It scared me since I'd occasionally indulged with him. They never showed you the lungs of someone who just smoked casually on the weekends, as a reward after a long week of work and not smoking. I pictured one pink lung and one black lung and imagined that was something I could live with.

We were about to wrap it up when he started, for the countless time for myself at least, the story of his father's passing. It was up at a cottage, which was on an island near Honey Harbour. He had to sea-doo the dead man in to shore strapped to his back because you can't get an ambulance to an island. He told us how the two life vests strapped together around him and his father had come loose and how he'd rode a good three minutes before noticing the dead man had completely fallen off.

He found him with a snapping turtle on his back, nibbling on his ears and, this being long before smartphones, didn't allow him to take a photo to show the rest of his family how funny it was and how he alone had to push the wet lifeless body back on the sea-doo, this time putting his father in front and wrapping his arms behind him as if teaching the corpse to ride.

We packed up, went back inside and straight to our closet. As we were about to fall asleep, the broom leaning between us, she asked, "Can you tell me a story?"

"You didn't enjoy the sea-doo one from earlier tonight?"

"It's what's keeping me awake."

"Fine. This one is called 'The Mermaid'.

"There was a mermaid that washed up on shore. She was middle-aged and not particularly pretty so no one cared. Though I'm sure she was attractive yesteryear, today she was not and today she made children cry and teenagers holler, all accept one man.

"The one man was very handsome and no one understood why he cared.

"When the magazine came to take pictures of them for their monthly 'Beauty and the Beast' column, he shooed them away from her rock.

"As the years passed, he became old and she stayed middle-aged. She had lied about being youthful and pretty once, for mermaids never change or age. They come into this world as is and stay as they came. The truth for one man was that he would age and die.

"The mermaid had never thought about him dying so in order to get ahead of it she made him leave.

"'You'll be old and probably sick soon. I can't sit on this rock holding your corpse till you rot.'

"'You could bury me.'

"'That's much worse.'

"'Worse than holding me till I rot?'

"'We're too different, one man, please leave, before I have to kill you. Mermaid tradition.'

"He left and probably died somewhere but the mermaid continued to wash up on various shores with no one caring like someone once had. The end."

"Who was your one man?" she asked.

"That story isn't about me."

"Not anymore it isn't."

She stumped me with that comment. Should I be more suspicious of her taking the only man who'd ever care of me? Maybe this Barbie doll wasn't as stupid as she looked, which was really quite stupid.

Over time, she became like a daughter to me, one of those mother-daughter relationships where you drink together. She introduced me to a game her and the girls used to play back at the factory.

"Sounds fun, I'll start. Never have I ever licked a kitchen floor," I said. She looked at me and drank.

"Never have I ever watched a porno." I liked how she added the 'o' on the end, the way it was intended. I took a long sip of my cocktail and told her about the internet.

"Never have I ever felt loved." I stirred my drink.

"Well don't make this sad," she said, but also didn't drink.

"Never have I ever had a threesome," she said as we looked at each other, then heard the front screen door open.

We whipped off each other's clothes – it's not hard to get off a pair of daisy dukes and tube tops, rolling them up or down our bodies – and pulled him into the bedroom. There was a lot of tossing from one side of the bed to the other. I felt like I was back on the conveyer belt and then I must have caught my plug on something as I started to deflate right between them.

No one really seemed to notice and they carried on with me, stuck between their thrusting bodies. They finished and peeled me off like an inconvenient sheet that had got caught in the action.

"I love you," he told her and I wanted to die.

"How was your day, Papi?" she replied and we all went to sleep.

The next morning, still naked, while making instant coffee in the kitchen, Claudia noticed my tattoo.

"I know, he wrote 'Daddy' on my foot, probably did it to you as well, it's a *Toy Story* reference, you're too young to get it."

"It's actually on your back."

I ran over to the mirror, to find the word 'whore' written on my back with a black sharpie.

"Oh," I replied.

"Is it written on mine?"

She turned around and her perfectly clear back bared no such slanderous graffiti.

It was becoming clear who his favourite was and with her only life mission being to please him, she had to go.

He had left us a list of chores for the day, the top priority being his precious pool. I told her to bring the skimmer and dive in. The bathing suit I had her wear had to be safety pinned in eight different spots as it was one left behind from his only portly human wife.

I thought I could lure her into the pool and the problem would solve itself. I mean of course she could get wet but she was never to be fully submerged. She carefully climbed up the ladder. I told her she looked good in the swimsuit and I saw a little spark as her toe touched the top of the water.

I held the skimmer just out of reach for her to grab and in she fell. She didn't quite float or sink, but was face down with her hands flapping in an attempt to grab the water. As I watched her flutter on the surface I wondered why I was working so hard to keep this man I hated, who treated me horribly, who stretched every single one of my holes without so much as a thank you and who had brought another woman into this house and tried to convince me that it was what I had wanted.

She managed to roll over and cried out, "Do you like that?" and, "You're a big growing boy."

I waited for a breeze then flung myself in her direction like a buoy.

"Grab on."

She started to vibrate and we wiggled our way to the edge.

We made it out and sat there staring at each other. Then he came home and somehow ended up at the bottom of the pool. The cops are still working on solving his mysterious death.

She got the house. He had changed the will when they secretly married but that didn't matter anymore. I headed south of our small town and went down to the water. I found a rock to sit on while I passed the time listening to the waves come in and out, waiting for someone to blow me up again.

~

Lauren Guyatt's Biography

Lauren Guyatt has worked for fifteen years as a second assistant director in film and television in Toronto, Canada, where she currently resides with her fiancé downtown in an overpriced but spacious apartment with their Doberman, Gonnie Goo Goo. While she prefers to work on comedic sitcoms, there is also a good mix of horror and fantasy she enjoys. She avoids hospital shows mainly due to the fluorescent lighting.

Lauren has been published many times in *The Feathertale Review* as well as their online publications. Her most recent stories, 'Dream Phone' and 'The Phone Call', were featured in issue #24.

She recently studied to become a yoga instructor while residing in Venice Beach, California, in 2020 in the hope of finding better balance in life.

She is set to begin filming a new show with the CBC (Canadian Broadcasting Corporation) in September 2021. She will continue to follow her passion of writing short stories and is working towards putting together a collection while continuing to grow in the television industry.

FML

Shortlisted story, by Jude Gray

"By the way, the cat's got dementia." The teen throws the statement out there as if she's just adding to a shopping list. *Buy milk and we're out of toothpaste and the cat's got dementia.*

"Eh, what? How do you know that?" I take a gulp of my coffee but it's too hot and scalds the roof of my mouth.

"Inappropriate eliminations." She flings open the back door. "Google it." She marches out of the house. The icy blast from the back door prompts me to get up and shut it as I do most days.

Google tells me that an 'inappropriate elimination' is when a cat starts avoiding its litter tray, instead doing the toilet in weird places. My phone pings. A text from the teen.

'Check the sink'

I check the sink. Inappropriate eliminations indeed. Both kinds. I sigh and reach for the disinfectant. The cat's got dementia and the teen's got attitude. I've got a dead-end job that I hate then I get to come home and pick up after Senile and Grumpy. As the teen would say, FML. This is not what I imagined being a grown-up would be like. I thought I'd have a job that I loved, a lively social life and I would be in control of it all. Instead I control nothing. Not even the kitchen sink.

FML.

Sink cleaned. Dishes washed. Dressed and out the door, stuffing cold toast into my mouth as I run to the bus stop. I make it by the skin of my toast-furred teeth but have to stand the whole way to the office. It's only as I'm shrugging my coat off and switching on my computer that I remember it's Tuesday and I'm delivering a presentation on 'communications in the social media age' and it starts in seven minutes. I click open my slides and pray that the PowerPoint fairy has magically populated them overnight but, sadly, I still only have a title page and a chirpy 'Any Qs?' page at the end. Six minutes to write my slides.

FML.

My phone buzzes. The teen.

'We're going on a trip to the national library and you didn't sign the letter'

What letter? Jesus, did I miss it? Five and half minutes for slides.

'Where is the letter?'

Maybe I can fix this.

'In my bag'

Ahh. I haven't seen the letter. I have the moral high ground but the problem remains. Five minutes. I phone the school, apologise and give verbal consent for the trip that is grudgingly accepted by the mafia that run the school reception and I'm left in no doubt that I've failed as a parent. Again. Three minutes. I grab a few quotes and memes from the internet and rush to the meeting room. I'm the last to arrive and have to endure the anguish of trying to link my laptop to the big screen while everyone watches me expectantly.

It's not my finest hour in the office. It might even be up there with the time that I told my boss I only needed to engage my brain once a week to do the job because it was so mind-numbingly dull that an untrained monkey could do it. That was after a regrettably long, liquid lunch in the pub. It took days of humble apologies and weeks of conspicuous hard work to recover. The look on my boss's face today tells me that today's presentation, or lack of it, is going to be even harder to recover from. It doesn't help that his boss was also in the room watching my garbled slides of memes and emoji. Luckily the teen is due to stay with her dad for the next seven days, which means I'll be free to make amends by coming in early and staying late. A show of working long hours is all it takes to be considered hard-working and committed to the job. Presence over substance, which can be a challenge for single parents. Sadly, that also means my plans to rekindle my social life this week will once again need to be put on hold.

My phone buzzes. It's the unreliable ex.

'Gonna have to cancel next week. Work. Sorry.'

Damn. Another text.

'Can you tell her for me?'

Great. So, I get to be the parent that breaks the bad news again. Cowardly as well as unreliable. FML.

I manage to avoid my boss for the rest of the day and escape the office a few minutes before five o'clock without having to listen to his lecture about time management and how he knows what it's like to juggle home and work responsibilities. He does, after all, have a dog. Well, a pug. Almost a dog.

My phone buzzes on the bus. The teen. She's starving. What's for dinner? Good question. Sometimes, I wish that I'd got a dog. I know that the fridge is virtually empty but there's definitely pasta in the cupboard. I try to remember if there's a jar of pesto. We could have pesto pasta. Again. I text the teen to check the cupboard for pesto but she replies instantly. In caps.

'I'M NOT HAVING PESTO PASTA AGAIN. NO WAY.'

Damn. My brain has reached capacity and I can't think of a single meal I can make with a bag of pasta and whatever else might be lurking in my cupboard. Nobody warns you that part of being a grownup means that you'll need to plan every single meal for the rest of your life. I decide to treat us to pizza and arrange to have a large pepperoni delivered. That should please the teen. Then she messages again.

'Going to Abby's for dinner. At least her mum feeds her.'

Large pizza for one. FML.

I'm watching re-runs for *Friends* on Netflix with the demented cat when the teen comes home. She throws herself down on the sofa next to me and starts tucking into the leftover pizza in the box on the coffee table.

"I thought Abby's mum made proper food?" I can't

resist saying.

She's just stuffed the best part of a slice of pizza in her mouth and it takes her a few moments to clear it and reply.

"She made mac and cheese but it was rubbish." She leans forward and grabs another slice. "Nothing like yours." She smiles at me through a mouthful of tomato and pepperoni.

My phone pings. It's my boss. His boss loved my presentation and wants me to deliver it again tomorrow to the heads of department. Apparently, memes and emoji are the future of communication and I've nailed it. He even sends me a picture of his pug wearing a ridiculous pink bowtie. I delete it but not before I send 'thumbs up' and 'laughing face' emoji.

"Can we watch the one where Ross can't flirt?" the teen asks, curling up against me. I nod and hand her the remote. I realise that this is as close as I will get to an apology.

We can hear the cat scratching in her litter tray in the hallway.

"Appropriate eliminations," we say as one and laugh.

LML. For a moment I love my life.

I'll tell her tomorrow about her dad cancelling.

~

Jude Gray's Biography

I am a writer who has been putting pen to paper and creating stories and poems for the past fifteen years. In the past five years my focus and commitment to writing has crystallised into a regular writing regime that has both improved the quality and quantity of my output, and also given me the pleasure of watching my stories develop and grow.

I've completed several novels and I've had a couple of short stories and poems published in small magazines, most recently in *The Selkie*. I live in Edinburgh and work part-time as a risk manager, which allows me regular writing time.

HACKED OFF

Shortlisted story, by Geoff Mead

George looked at his hands on the keyboard. In the pale, early morning light, it was hard to make out every detail, but he was sure his skin was getting more translucent. *Bollocks*, he thought. *I wonder how much longer I've got before I can see right through them. That would be weird, but it's bound to happen before too long. If I don't stop doing this, then I'll be completely invisible one day. I don't mind strangers looking right through me when we pass in the street, but I don't know what I'll do if I can't see myself.*

He reached out until his left hand found the mug of

tea on the bedside table, then brought his right hand round until he had the mug in both hands. It was his favourite, bought years ago at the Shetland Film Festival, when people still wanted him to make public appearances and he didn't mind being the centre of attention. It was imprinted with an obscure movie pun: 'Yippee ki-yay Muckle Flugga.' It was his test of whether someone was his sort of person or not. If they couldn't make the association between Bruce Willis's obscene catch phrase in *Die Hard* and the name of a rocky outcrop off the Isle of Unst, then no matter how interesting they were in other respects, he had to let them go. Life was both too short and too long to associate with people like that.

He swallowed a mouthful of the hot tea and groped for the ginger biscuits, dunked one until it drooped precariously, lifted it above his head and lowered it into his mouth. One false move and there would be yet another ginger stain on the sheets. He took it into his waiting maw, like a goldfish sucking down a piece of soggy bread from the surface of the pond, then pushed in the remaining, un-dunked half. Soft *and* crunchy. The habit of a lifetime, his own invention, once the scourge of his mother's desperately polite tea parties. "George, I wish you wouldn't do that."

How often he had heard those words, first from his mother and then from each of his three or was it four ex-wives. He imagined that the phrase had been passed on from one to another, originally as a wedding gift from his mother and then as part of successive divorce settlements. *Fuck it*, George thought. *Solitary confinement isn't easy but it's a small price to pay for not being constantly disapproved of.*

He finished his tea, demolishing a second ginger nut

in the same manner as the first in the process.

His hands, he noticed, had resumed their flapping over the keyboard, fingers alighting more or less at random on the keys. Well, not exactly at random, but certainly without any conscious intention. He looked at the screen to see what it was he had been writing. Another Katie Price novel? The surprisingly well-written autobiography of an illiterate footballer? A blazingly original new novel by some washed-up old Booker Prize winner? Whatever it was, it didn't make much sense.

He decided to let his hands carry on without him, as they usually did. His waking hours were far too precious to waste on actually thinking about the guff he churned out for other people under the soubriquet of Habakkuk Penworthy.

The name had been his agent Tabitha's idea.

"Is that Habakkuk?" was her opening line when he'd made the mistake of answering the phone. He'd seen who was calling and should have known better. Agents never bring good news.

"Who the fuck is Habakkuk?"

"*Old Testament* prophet. Wrote the eighth of the twelve books of the prophets."

"What's that got to do with me?"

"Have you ever read the Book of Habakkuk?"

"No."

"Nor has anybody else, darling."

"Ha, bloody ha."

"I'm afraid no one wants to pick up your manuscript," said Tabitha. "It's prophetic and brilliant, of course. You and I know that, but there isn't a publisher in the land who thinks anybody will ever buy it."

"Too dystopian?"

"Too hopeful."

"Well, how am I going eat? I'm a writer. It's all I can do. I need some money. I'm earning fuck all at the moment."

"True enough, Habakkuk. But at least you get to keep eighty-five percent of fuck all. My fifteen percent ain't going to butter no parsnips, I can tell you."

"Why parsnips?"

"No idea, darling. But I can tell you they ain't going to get buttered. Unless..."

"Unless what?"

"Have you ever thought of putting your mighty talent to work in service of people who don't really have anything to say but could sell a gazillion books if they did?"

"Celebrities?"

"Celebs. Influencers. Public figures. Politicians. That sort of thing."

"Bollocks."

"It pays very well, Habakkuk. Enough to keep you in ginger biscuits for the rest of your days. You can still write your own scintillating stuff on the side. I'll keep trying to sell it, of course. There's bound to be a niche small enough, somewhere."

"How much?"

"It's usually a fixed fee. I could probably get you five grand a pop."

"I'm not a prostitute, Tabitha."

"You'd have to suck a lot of dicks to earn five grand."

"Where did you get such a potty mouth?"

"Hanging around writers like you," she said. "Now, do you want to eat or not?"

"I suppose I could try doing one. Five grand would come in very handy."

"That's my boy. I'll send you something over this afternoon. I've got a few autobiographies that need writing before the public forgets who the hell they are about. There's *Up Yours: My Life as the World's Leading Proctologist, Fairy Dust and Pixie Boots: 50 Years as a Pantomime Dame,* or *Grabbed by the Balls: The Lure of Snooker.* Which one do you fancy?"

"I can't quite believe I'm saying this," George had replied, "but I think *Grabbed by the Balls* would be the least painful option."

"Wonderful. I'll draw up the contract straight away."

"Just make sure that my real name is nowhere to be seen. I don't want my ex-wives revelling in how low I've sunk since they left me."

"Leave it with me, darling. I'll think of something."

George leaned back on the pillow and grimaced as he remembered the birth of his shameful secret career. He still sometimes thought about writing his own stuff, but his fingers no longer responded to his own mind. After years of undignified labour, they clearly wanted as little to do with him as possible. *Maybe that's why I'm fading away*, he thought. *Every time I hit the keys, another bit of my soul is destroyed.*

It's alright for Tabitha Granville-sodding-Smythe, he thought. *All she has to do is sign the contracts and rake in the cash. I reckon she has loads of us tucked away in that* Walpurgisnacht *of an agency: nocturnal, unseen, productive souls on their way to the seventh circle of Hell. Fifteen percent of the fruits of our collective misery is more than enough to fund her Chipping Norton lifestyle. She's an unprincipled, avaricious, literary gang master, throwing scraps into the cell that is my life*, he decided, unable to stop himself enjoying his own metaphor. They never spoke on the phone these days.

If she wanted something, a message would pop up in the top right-hand corner of his computer screen. Usually, it was to remind him of an impending deadline, reinforced by a copy of the penalty clause for late delivery.

George held his hands up to the shaft of light forcing its way into his bedroom through a crack in the grubby curtains. He could see the assemblages of carpals, metacarpals and phalanges as clearly as if he'd been looking at an X-ray. "This has to stop," he said out loud. "I can't stand it any longer." He gritted his teeth, grabbed his left wrist in his right hand and forced it toward the keyboard. "There's only one way out for a ghost writer who has had enough."

His left hand curled involuntarily into a ball as what was left of his body's instinct for survival kicked in. He slid his right hand along from his left wrist and straightened his left forefinger with all the force he could muster. If he let the moment pass, he knew he would never forgive himself. He stabbed desperately at the keys with his pinioned left forefinger until, on the fourth attempt, he hit the escape key... and Habakkuk Penworthy disappeared forever, taking George with him.

When the authorities broke into the house to see what had happened, the only sign that either Habakkuk or George had ever been there was an empty Shetland Film Festival mug beside the bed.

They weren't George's kind of people.

Nobody got the joke.

Muckle Fluggas.

~

Geoff Mead's Biography

Geoff Mead lives in a house, appropriately named Folly Cottage, in Kingscote, Gloucestershire. The first thing he ever wanted to do as a child aged eight was to write stories. Unfortunately, it took another fifty years before he discovered anything worth writing about.

In the past few years he has authored six published books of fiction, non-fiction, poetry and memoir. With the help of his trusty, canine companion Captain Midnight, he writes an irregular blog.

As an organisational consultant, keynote speaker and workshop leader, for the past two decades he has taken his work on narrative leadership onto the shop floors and into the boardrooms of blue-chip companies, charities, universities and government departments.

Geoff also performs traditional stories at international festivals and storytelling clubs and runs story-based workshops in the UK and as far afield as Spain, Canada and Japan.

Blog: www.cominghometostory.com

IT'S NOT EASY BEING AN ECTOPLASMIC MUTANT ABOMINATION

Shortlisted story, by Bryant Phillips

Hi. My name is Aaaaawhatisthatthing. At least I assume it is. That's what people scream at me whenever they see me. I'm an experimental creation gone wrong with a guilt complex and the physical visage of cottage cheese.

I was created by Dr Kip Rockwell, scientist. He was working in the lab late one night, when my eyes beheld an eerie sight. It was me of course, as I beheld my monstrous form, my first moment of cognition.

"Doctor." It was Dr Rockwell's assistant, Debra. I wasn't yet aware her name was Debra, just as I wasn't aware of Dr Rockwell's name either. I was too busy staring at the oozing stump that was apparently my hand.

I saw Dr Rockwell whip his glasses off and turn his chiselled features toward her. There was a small window in my secured chamber and the sounds outside echoed in it. "Deb. Did you get me that scotch I requested?"

"No, doctor, it's the radiation gauge. The levels are off the scale."

I prodded my face to see if I had a nose like they did. There was a gaping, festering maw instead, spewing vapours and caustic excretions. My mouth, I supposed.

Dr Rockwell gave a laugh that even I could tell was pretentious. "Oh Deb, that's just your overactive woman's imagination getting the best of you, and all those emotions. Everything is under control. I'm a scientist."

I appeared to be attached to a large machine by a series of tubes. I gave an experimental tug.

"But doctor, the ray shielding on those doors..."

"Will hold." Dr Rockwell got up. I watched him sidle up to Debra and grab her around the waste. Even I knew his behaviour was all wrong, and I'd been self-aware for all of five minutes. "Besides, we have more important business."

"Shouldn't we turn off the electrostatic oscillating

mass spectro-gravimeter inhibitor first?"

"Only after I get a kiss." He dipped her below the control panel.

I was frankly appalled. I seemed to have been gifted a basic working knowledge of the world from the doctor, and at that moment it was working against him. In a fit of rage at the insensitivity and unprofessionalism of this chauvinist, I pulled hard at the tubes and managed to disconnect them. With no general reaction from the humans outside my chamber, I began banging on the sealed doors. Only then did Dr Rockwell's head pop up.

"Zounds, what in God's name...?"

I banged again and was surprised to see the glass break. Apparently, these chunky stumps for hands were stronger than I realised. One more smash, and the steel doors came completely off their hinges. I was free. That was remarkably easy.

"Debra, get behind me."

"Doctor, we need to call someone. The government. The police."

"No, I can handle this. I'll use my male intuition."

Dr Rockwell put a wooden tube in his mouth — a pipe, my brain correctly identified — as he regarded me. For reasons I couldn't explain, this nonchalant gesture had the effect of calming my rage and making me realise the mess I'd created. I looked at the broken doors beneath me. Could I fix those?

"I expect you're wondering why you were made. It's simple — science should always be pushed to its ethical limits for the sake of science. That's basic logic."

I grabbed both doors and tried squeezing them together in their original place. They crumpled like aluminium cans. I tried picking up all the shards of glass.

No fingers. Curses.

"My name is Dr Rockwell, and I created you. That makes me your master."

I slowly processed what Dr Rockwell was saying. I stood, and a sudden emotion overcame my glutinous mass as I reckoned with my first profound realisation – this man was the reason I was alive. I may have only possessed an elementary knowledge of what a father was, but the doctor seemed the closest approximate, and if I knew how to talk I'd have cried it out loud. Instead, I made a sort-of repugnant bubbly croak and tried to embrace him.

This did not lead to a good outcome.

He shot me. I experienced pain for the first time and didn't relish it. I was sent reeling and crashed into the wall.

"Debra, don't just stand there, call the police."

I tried to steady myself, but being still unaccustomed to my brutish strength, my arm smashed right through the wall. I observed with horror the sizable hole, and with equal horror the hole in my chest where the bullet had lodged. Dr Rockwell was brandishing his gun like he meant to use it again and, in a flash, I assessed my own danger and weighed the pros and cons of remaining here. Pros: my master, my creator, the reason for my existence, was here. Cons: he shot me. I chose the wall.

Ploughing through it like a bulldozer, I emerged from the rubble stricken with guilt and blinded from the lights that shone over the parking lot. Several figures were issuing from a small booth at the far end, and even from a distance I could see them holding guns like Dr Rockwell's. I tried to explain that this was a misunderstanding and I'd repair the wall myself, once I developed fingers, but a glancing shot off the pulsating secretion that was my shoulder made me flee in terror.

These creatures were monsters. Didn't they at least want to hear me out first? Have some civil discourse and talk about our feelings before a group hug and a nightcap? I ran through a fence, charged down a street, leapt over a Cadillac, trampled a stop sign, nearly flattened a dog and stumbled drunken and disorderly into an outdoor movie theatre.

And that was where I earned the name Aaaaawhatisthatthing.

I don't think it helped that the people were watching a film remarkably similar to my current predicament, featuring a beast (rather handsome, I thought) rampaging through a small town in clear distress from the reactionist humans attacking him. I felt for the beast, pausing a moment to watch, although I found I had to constantly wipe dripping ooze out of my beady eyes. I probably viewed a total of two minutes before the screaming began. Actual screaming, not the film's.

They got in their cars and began driving erratically while I stood in their midst, weighing my options. Pros: if I stayed, I could finish the film, maybe even try befriending these humans. Cons: they could shoot me. I heard the sirens approaching and chose my own safety again, although a part of me felt these acts of self-preservation were cowardly, and perhaps I owed it to the humans to make amends for driving them into fits of all-consuming terror. I'd make them something pretty later on, maybe weave them a gift basket. Once I developed fingers.

It happened that the outdoor cinema abutted a swamp. I lurched into it, pushing through the muck and mire, aware that the sirens had stopped, and wisely found a large stump to hide behind just as a powerful beam of light was cast upon the marsh, sweeping back and forth to find me. After a moment, the light turned off, and the sounds of the humans faded shortly thereafter. I was left alone, a creature of filth in a bog of stagnation, with my fear and self-loathing threatening to overcome me.

Then I met Her.

She was a primordial swamp thing, the very manifestation of the place she called home, a callous and wretched scum of villainy whose life of isolation and persecution at the hands of the humans had twisted her into a vengeful lusus naturae of unspeakable horror. I was smitten by her immediately. We couldn't exactly speak to each other, but I called her Corpse Flower.

What she saw in me I couldn't say – perhaps it was a long-sought ally to overthrow the humans. She circled me, inspecting me, tossing her long tendrils of fungus and grime out of her nightmarish face with fingers that looked like spindly branches. I may have bubbled and churned a tad exuberantly when she brushed them against my back. All I could think about was somehow growing fingers so we could hold hands.

She pointed ominously toward the far side of the swamp, clearly formulating a plan. We began with a warm-up, targeting a group of teenagers who had unwisely rolled their car to the edge of a bluff overlooking the swamp. The male, accompanied by noisome pop music, appeared to be making solicitous advances upon the female. This made me think of Dr Rockwell, and I had no qualms when Flower bade me wrap my arms around the car from behind and flip it upside down, though I made sure to jiggle the passenger side so the young lady fell out before upturning it. It was the gentlemanly thing to do.

From thereon, Flower took the lead. I must confess her bloodlust was exhilarating. Whereas I would meekly crush a bicycle and maybe tip over a dumpster, she would shriek like a harpy and plough through a convenience store like it was made of origami paper. I admired her commitment to her work, even as I still found myself wrestling with the morality of it all. I even made sure to pile and sort the wares once she'd finished eviscerating the store.

In one instance we wandered into a forest and chanced upon a group of children dressed in matching uniforms about a roaring fire. Their adult master appeared to be trying to scare the children with spooky stories, which seemed a poor teaching method for impressionable minds. Flower, of course, had to make an entrance, bursting from the bushes like a rabid badger in heat. I took great pains to apologise to the screaming kids while surreptitiously grabbing a chunk of goo from my midsection and flinging it at their loathsome adult master. I could apparently do that.

When the area cleared, Flower and I had a moment together, alone by the fire. We both found it captivating, being the first fire we'd ever seen, and the hot dogs the kids had left roasting were the most delicious food I'd ever had (and also the only food I'd ever had). As we enjoyed its warmth, I stared into Flower's bulging dragonfly-like eyes and thought I saw a deep longing. Whether it was for me, the fire, or the desire to exterminate all of humanity, I couldn't tell.

A minute more and she was ready to go, issuing a cry like a million damned souls from Hell and stampeding through the woods while I trailed behind, admiring her bloated figure. We issued from the woods onto a hilltop overlooking the city strip, large neon lights and slow-cruising automobiles beckoning us like a moth to a flame. Strictly speaking there weren't any flames yet, but Flower didn't take long to start them, grabbing a fuel tank at a gas station and tossing it in the air like a hacky-sack. That sort of act tends to attract a lot of attention.

I could see where this was going. I may not have been sentient very long, and I was still extraordinarily green (putrid green), but I recognised a doomed love affair when I saw one. As sirens came blaring from all directions, I stood upon the tightrope of indecision, balancing between my desire to withdraw somewhere safe with Flower and my endless adoration for her artistry of destruction. I privately knew she'd never settle for anything less than 'kill or be killed'. I personally wouldn't mind 'give love a chance'.

She rushed the first police car that arrived on the scene, hurling it down the main drag. I stopped to gently rescue a birds' nest from a nearby tree, though without fingers (lord those would have been nice) I couldn't seem to accomplish this without uprooting the entire tree and setting it outside Flower's little war zone. This was to be my last gentile act.

The bullets started whizzing like a summer of cicadas. We retreated to a water tower, the largest building in town. Ladders are meant for humans, so we wrapped our limbs about the poles and shimmied up, ungracefully. We reached the top, and Flower began attempting to push it over. I watched the multiple spotlights illuminate the love of my life (such as it was), and everything seemed to go suddenly mute, as though a blanket were cast over the calamity below. I took a breath, held it, relished the moment.

Our doomed romance came to an end there, atop the world. I was filled with more lead than a hundred pound ballast weight. I never saw my love fall – in my private fantasies, she's still out there, sticking it to the man (or woman, she seemed indiscriminate), impervious to anything and everything, a beacon for us lost souls.

My last memories from that day were lying on the ground, as Dr Rockwell approached. In the flashing of red and white lights I saw him retrieve a case from his pocket, open it and settle the pipe between his lips as he regarded me, broken and dying before him.

"Sir, what in God's name is that?" an officer asked him as my vision narrowed.

"A failure, sergeant. A glorious failure."

*

I expect you're wondering if my story concluded there. Dr Rockwell had other plans.

As I recall these memories, I look around the lab from my new prison, encased in a glass jar. For you see, I am now but a brain, a pulsing blob of wrinkled pink with a stem and two eyes attached by sinewy optical nerves. Once I was a thing of horror and primordial sludge, a hulking titan with a heart of gold. Now that heart has withered and died, and I'm left to brood and simmer like a bubbling cauldron of cynicism.

But once again, Dr Rockwell has underestimated my strength. I can feel power rising through my cranial faculties, and it won't take long before I can conceivably stretch my newfound telepathic abilities and burst free, ready to seek revenge upon those who subjected me to this cursed and degenerate status. Gone is the sweetness and childlike innocence. I shall dominate the minds of the human monsters and enslave them to my will, starting with Dr Rockwell. They shall be my puppets and I their puppet master. The lightning and thunder rend the sky apart as the rain lashes upon the window, an echo of my swelling cry for retribution.

Soon... and this time, I'll get fingers.

~

Bryant Phillips' Biography

I'm a full-time dad from Seattle attempting to reinvent myself post-pandemic as an aspiring author. I'm currently working on a series with my father, Doug, an accomplished author with six published books, while simultaneously working on my own novel and various pet projects like this one. I only do comedy, so lord help me if you don't like my humour, and lord bless you if you do.

NO MOJITOS IN SIBERIA

Shortlisted story, by L M Rees

I was Marco Polo at the foot of the Silk Road, Columbus at the mouth of the ocean, Laika the dog hot-footing it onto *Sputnik Two*. Most freelance researchers would give their left kidney to do a job like this: I'd been commissioned to spend a month in Siberia researching shamans. Even though the temperature was minus twenty-four Celsius when I arrived, freezing my testicles off still beat being tethered to a desk doing market research for dog food companies, or suchlike. My excitement about this expedition was positively volcanic.

Was. Past tense. Not so much anymore.

A lot can change in a fortnight.

Today, my thermometer screams at me that it's minus thirty-two. I open the front door of the guesthouse and the cold hits me in the face like an industrial custard pie. One made of lead with rusty bolts and screws protruding at inconvenient angles. The freezing air shoots me in the eyeballs, the nostrils, down to my lungs. The warming effect of my thermal layers, down coat and snow boots already starts to diminish, and at least three of my senses refuse to operate. I wonder what the suicide rate is among the locals.

In addition to the inclement weather, I've done no work of use during the past fortnight, and not through lack of trying. It turns out that genuine shamans are more elusive than the yeti. I've already reached the halfway point of my expedition, and my client will soon expect me to send an update. She is paying me more than I usually earn in six months, so failure is not an option. I try to evoke the spirit of Columbus, Amundsen, Sir Hillary and Tenzing Norgay, or anyone else I can think of, and set out to give this project one last shot.

I crunch through the snow towards the bus stop to meet my translator and guide, Katishka, an old-school, vodka-swilling Babushka with a witch's cackle and wisps of white hair that peep out from her headscarf. On arriving at the bus stop, Katishka is nowhere to be seen, so I jump up and down to keep myself alive. Finally, I see a figure in the distance. I pray it isn't my guide, although she is clearly recognisable, and the sight of two horses plodding behind her is not one I welcome.

"Katishka, hello. Nice to see you." I look pointedly at

my watch. "Who are your two friends?"

"These are our transports."

She hands me a rope attached to the larger of the two horses.

"What's his name?"

"Horse."

"What's your horse's name?"

"Horse."

"I didn't know you had horses."

"I borrowed them. We must rush, Derek. Get on."

I think better of pointing out the more obvious solution to getting to our shaman on time: Katishka arriving punctually.

"What do you mean get on? I thought we were going by bus."

She laughs. "Why do you think that?"

"Because you told me to meet you at this bus stop."

"There is no bus here since 1989. During Socialist era, bus takes you everywhere. Now there is just bus stops. We must go by horse. Shaman lives down very small lane."

"I can't ride a horse."

"Why can you not ride horse? All good men ride horse."

"I've never learned."

She cackles in a way that makes me feel emasculated. "You won't get anywhere in Siberia if you can't ride horse."

I'm not getting anywhere in Siberia anyway. "But I can't ride. I don't know how."

"Get on."

I watch her mount her beast, then she chuckles unsupportively as I clamber onto mine.

"During Socialist era, even babies could ride horse.

Follow me."

I try kicking, like they do in cowboy films, but the horse doesn't budge. Katishka grabs the rope attached to its bridle and drags us along behind her.

"Sometimes, Derek," she gives me a big, wrinkly smile, "you are like child."

I take it as a compliment, although I suspect it wasn't meant as one.

During the past fortnight Katishka has arranged no fewer than seven interviews with shamans, none of which have come to fruition. One was so drunk on fermented mare's milk, he could barely remember his name, let alone species. Another had moved to Moscow three weeks earlier to study medicine, while another answered almost every question with, "I cannot tell you. That information is for shamans only." Two had mysteriously disappeared and the final pair sweet-talked us until I paid the so-called interview fee, then they scarpered. I resorted to reading about shamans in the local library with the aid of a large dictionary and attending a touristy folklore show featuring an actor pretending to be a shaman healing a chap in the audience who'd clearly been planted. I sincerely hope today's shaman isn't as off-piste as the others.

"So, Katishka, tell me about the shaman."

"He come from very long line of shamans. His parents, grandparents, grand-grand-parents, grand-grand-grand-parents..."

I get the picture but let her continue.

"His name is Ayatas, means very good friend. Honest friend. He is intelligent man. He has great knowledges. He will be very good for you to interview."

This sounds great; however, I should check a couple of facts.

"Is he an alcoholic?"

"No."

"Will he answer my questions?"

"Yes."

Horse Two, as I've named my steed, stamps its hooves, and I almost fall off.

"Does he still live there, or has he moved to Moscow to become a doctor?"

"Cheeky, Derek."

That's good enough for me.

"After we interview nice shaman, I will very soon go to live in Cuba."

When not extolling the virtues of Marxism-Leninism and reminiscing the glory days of Communism, Katishka has spent the past fortnight speaking yearningly about Cuban beaches, classic American cars, cigars and mojitos. She once met a Cuban man called Juan at a communist exchange in Lensk, and now she's waiting for her husband to die so she can go to Cuba to be with him.

"Cuba is most blissful place on Earth, Derek."

I look at the endless snow, feel the wind biting into my bones, and suddenly find the thought of sitting on a Cuban beach painfully tempting. Tantalising images of mojitos, palm trees and the relative pleasures of sunburn dance before my frozen eyelashes.

"And my husband will soon expire, thank Lord." She crosses herself. "We are here."

Katishka stops and Horse Two almost head-butts Horse One's bony behind. I am very much looking forward to meeting the shaman and finally getting my first proper interview under my belt. What I'm not looking forward to, however, is dismounting. My legs are numb, my hands don't move, and my arse fell off a couple of miles back. I now deeply regret never having learned to ride, although I doubt giving this apocalyptic pony a gentle tap and saying 'walk on' would do much good. Katishka jumps off her beast with the nimbleness of a teenage equestrian while I roll off mine, and since my legs have meanwhile turned into cotton wool, I promptly collapse in the snow.

"Get up, Derek. We need to make good impression with shaman."

I try moving, but my legs don't cooperate. "Just a moment." I punch my calves and thighs to get them working again. Horse Two looks as if it wants to help out by kicking me.

"Hurry up, Derek. We will be late."

"I was waiting at that bus stop for more than twenty minutes."

"And I was riding like child at fairground so you could follow my speed. Get off the snow." I hoist myself up and Katishka gives me a wide, leathery smile. "Good boy. Follow me."

She ties the horses to a tree, and we walk — well, she walks and I hobble — down a path so tiny I suspect it was built by squirrels.

"Hurry up and do interview, Derek, so I can go live in Cuba."

"May I join you?"

She ignores me and struts towards the wooden hut before us.

Not only is this the most generously paid commission I've worked on, but it is also the most mysterious. My client has given me minimal information, other than instructions to interview as many shamans as possible and to write a report on their rituals, ceremonies, trances, and consultations. I suspect she intends on setting up business as a quack, but felt it wasn't my place to question her. Don't bite the hand that feeds you, and all that.

Katishka opens the door of the hut without knocking and steps inside.

'*Zdravstvuyte*,' says the sole occupant, a small-built, kindly-looking young man, sitting at a wooden table, tearing apart a large loaf of bread with hands that clearly haven't been washed in a decade. We nod our hellos, and he and Katishka exchange words in very fast, mumbling Russian.

"He says we able to sit down."

The tiny wooden stools do nothing to ease the stiffness in my legs, but at least the log burner saves me from cryonic suspension. I ask if it's polite to strip off a layer or four.

The man nods and points to his chest. "Ayatas," he says. "Ayatas."

I take off my hat, scarf, coat and fleece. "I'm Derek. Pleased to meet you."

We shake hands, then he reaches for three small glasses and a bottle from a shelf and pours clear liquid into each.

"Home-made vodka," says Katishka.

"*Spasibo*," I say, and Ayatas looks pleased that I've made an effort to speak Russian, although I don't know much more than that. The vodka tastes pleasant enough, but Katishka has got me thinking about mojitos and balmy sea air. I wholeheartedly want to do a good job and I endeavour to persevere to the very end, but the sad truth is that if any more interviews backfire, I may have to consider aborting this project altogether.

"Ayatas ask why you want to come to Siberia. He thinks you very adventure-ful."

"Thanks, Katishka. Only this morning, I fancied myself as a bit of a Marco Polo or Christopher Columbus, or even that true Russian hero, Laika the dog."

Katishka chortles. "Laika died in space rocket, and Christopher Columbus did not discover America. That was Viking Leif Eriksson."

She translates for Ayatas and they laugh at my expense.

"And Marco Polo maybe is worse. Many people believe his travel writings are fake."

She translates, they giggle again, but she's actually given me an idea, just in case this interview does not go according to plan. I take out my notebook, pen and voice recorder and ask Katishka if it's OK to begin. She nods. I start with a warm-up question, just to get Ayatas talking.

"Does he like living here?"

"Yes, he says he used to live with whole family, parents, grandparents in big house several kilometres away, but he is here alone now. He likes it. He does not even want to find wife."

"He has no children?"

"No children."

I don't picture shamans as family men anyway. I reckon communicating with the spirits doesn't complement changing nappies and assembling toy train sets. He seems happy to talk, though, for which I find myself feeling unnaturally grateful.

"So, Ayatas, can you give me some general information about the type of shamanism you practice."

Katishka translates the question, I get my pencil ready on a blank page, Ayatas replies.

"He says he doesn't know anything about

shamanism."

"He can tell me anything, any small piece of information is useful."

They talk again then she translates, "He says he knows nothing. He is not interested."

Katishka's hands are clasped firmly on her lap, she gazes downwards, deliberately avoiding eye contact.

"What does he mean he's not interested? Katishka, you told me he was a shaman."

They speak again. "He says he is not shaman. I am sorry, Derek. I think I was given wrong informations. It is mistake. He thinks you are here to ask about his life in Siberia."

"Yes, his life as a shaman. I've ridden here through inhumane temperatures on that bloody horse for this." I take a deep breath and lower my voice. "Does he know anything at all? I'll take any information I can."

They speak once again. Ayatas seems to be chatting away amicably but Katishka looks anxious. The idea Katishka inadvertently gave me when talking about Marco Polo starts whirring around my mind like a snowstorm.

"He told me his father was shaman, and his grandfather and his grand-grandfather. But he is not shaman, never interested, no talent for shamanism. He says you should speak to his parents. They know everything. His father very important shaman, healed many people."

Now we're getting somewhere. "Where can I find his parents?"

They exchange a few words, then she says, "They are dead."

"Both of them?"

"Yes."

"What about healing?"

They talk again. "He told me when he is ill, he prefers to go to hospital to see real doctor."

"And communicating with the spirits?"

"He says he cannot prove spirits exist, so he not yet happy to believe."

I feel dizzy. "Thank him for his time." I stand up, put my outdoor clothes back on, shake Ayatas by the hand, and step outside to face the freezing wall of extreme low temperatures, disappointment and panic. I've spent the entire fortnight chasing my tail and not one genuine shaman have I found. I now face a forty-minute trek on a demon horse in minus thirty-two plus the wind-chill factor back to a redundant bus stop, followed by a twenty-minute walk to an almost empty guesthouse to write up my notes on absolutely nothing. Why couldn't I have been sent to Cuba instead, or any place with beaches and temperatures above zero?

I now have to make a decision and there are three options. The least desirable is confessing to my client, quitting the project and losing all the money. The second choice is staying in Siberia and persevering with a stiff upper lip. The third option is jetting to Cuba on the next available flight, staying there for the remainder of the project's duration, and making up the report as I sip rum cocktails on the beach. I could just fake it, like Marco Polo might have done, while hoping my reputation for research and discovery will be made with the same ill-deserved good luck as Columbus. My client wouldn't know where I am, and it's not as if her intentions are entirely virtuous. It's tempting, but a last resort. I really want to choose option two.

Katishka follows me silently towards the horses when I am suddenly hit with one final idea, one last straw I can grasp at before giving up on the expedition and pegging it to the nearest Air Cubana ticket office.

I turn to Katishka, and through the howl of the icy wind, ask, "What about his grandparents and great-grandparents?"

"They are also dead."

Bollocks.

~

L M Rees' Biography

L M Rees writes darkly comic and historical fiction, as well as non-fiction about Asian music and film. Her book *Mongolian Film Music: Tradition, Revolution and Propaganda* was published by Ashgate/Routledge in 2015 (re-issued in 2020). She has an MA in creative writing with distinction, and has won the *Writers' Forum* monthly short story competition for her story 'Fast Train to Zion'. She has previously worked as a teacher of rock and classical music, an English teacher in Germany and Slovakia, a researcher in Mongolia and Wales, and a TV extra for several Welsh-language programmes (which involved freezing to near-death in swimwear on a beach near Cardiff one February). She has now opted for a quieter and warmer working life as a librarian. She lives in a small house by the sea, and spends her free time doing yoga and hoping the sea level doesn't rise too much.

RANDOM

Shortlisted story, by Tony Kirwood

Perhaps it was the ostrich feather tickling her eye that distracted Kamila. On the other hand it may have been Mr Darcy's stern brows looking down on her, or simply that her satin slippers were so darn skiddy. But on the second skip of the gavotte over she went, landing on her knees on the ballroom floor.

"Sod it." The words shot from her lips before she could stop them.

Kamila put her hand over her mouth. No one in Jane Austen swore. What would Mr Darcy think? "Stop it," she told herself. "He's not thinking anything. He's a robot."

A robot, though, who leant down and gracefully held out a hand to her.

"Miss Bennet, this is most unfortunate. May I fetch you a posset?"

"No, it's cool," she stammered. Why couldn't she come out with something more Austenesque?

He – she couldn't bear to think of it as *it* – gave one of his saturnine smiles and raised her hand in readiness for the next figure. Her heart fluttering, she turned out her toe.

Down the line from Darcy, Mr Rochester, Heathcliff and Prince Albert ducked and twirled. With their magnificent whiskers, muscular chests and silvery buttons, they looked the cream of nineteenth century manhood. 'State of the art robotics,' the History Parcs brochure had said. 'The synthetic partners we provide for our women's weekends are built like bulls but dance like gazelles. They are receptive to suggestion and extremely hygienic.'

So unlike men, thought Kamila.

The women were all proper humans and, to be honest, a bit of a let-down. Catherine Earnshaw was a ledger clerk in her fifties. Queen Victoria was a loud Texan blonde. Only Jane Eyre was remotely cool, but then she was being role-played by Kamila's best friend Babz, whose idea it had been to bring Kamila along with her. Babz knew the ropes. She had put on a dab of lipstick, let a strand of hair from her severe bun dangle alluringly over her cheek and undone the top button of her drab governess's gown.

Kamila felt a soft vibration from within her reticule. She had been clutching it like a lifeline. She turned away so Darcy couldn't see her and pulled out the phone. It was Scott. She swore quietly. She'd told her husband not to call.

"Hey, babe. The washex. How do you get it to do cottons?"

Why were men so useless? "I told you, Scott. Blue icon followed by your personal password. You've not forgotten it?"

He'd have chosen a beer brand, she thought. *Or a football team.*

"No. It's you. Kamila."

She couldn't suppress a pang of guilt. Scott, typically, kept on talking.

"How's the business convention, babe?"

"It's alright. Bit boring to be honest. Look, I'm in the middle..."

She became aware of a short fleshy figure standing in front of her, his blue shirt embellished by a badge: 'Nevil. IT Support.' His pink face was a contortion of annoyance and apology.

"Look, I'm sorry, but no technology in the ballroom. It upsets the robots' sequencing. I'll have to ask you to put that away. Sorry."

With a sigh Kamila shoved the phone back into the reticule.

"These XG3 Series 10s have got amazingly complex programming." He wasn't half droning on. "Nineteenth century language, attitudes, morals, the lot. But if you upset the algorithms by going outside the parameters, there's a danger they could go random and you wouldn't want that."

They'd said the same thing in the contract. Stay

within the characters. No anachrothingies. She yawned.

Nevil froze Darcy by pressing something at the back of his neck. The face sprang up to reveal a pudding of foamy material studded with tiny beads of light. Kamila turned away. She couldn't bear to watch it.

"No damage done this time. Lucky." Nevil pulled down the face and pressed Darcy's neck button. The tall figure came back to life and made a stately bow to Kamila.

"Yay," she said. She had him back. Now she must work at the situation more. Her tetchy exchange with Scott had made her suddenly determined to make the most of her time with someone a bit more... what was the word? Alpha, that was it.

The music finished. He walked to the side of the room and, awkwardly, she accompanied him. How could she break through his aloofness? Coquettish winks and flirtatious smiles were out of her range.

"Sorry if I'm a bit clumsy," she muttered.

"Miss Bennet," said Mr Darcy, "the elegance of your carriage makes me quite oblivious to any slight slip on the dance floor."

"Why, Mr Darcy," she said, "that's totally, er, awesome."

"And your conversation is but the least of your delights." Scott would never say anything like that.

Nevil had scuttled away. Staff were not encouraged to linger in the ballroom. It spoiled the effect for the clients.

But though Mr Darcy's words were warm his manner remained stiff. The conversation petered out and she could find no way of resuming it. No way worthy of Elizabeth Bennet, anyway.

*

"There are so few decent men around these days. It's natural to fall for a 'bot." Babz sipped her vodka crème. "Sensible, even."

The bar at History Parcs offered end of the day relief from the ballroom, library and conservatoire. With the robots switched off and encased, the women had swapped their regency dresses for jeans and had flopped into the sofas.

Kamila shut her eyes and pictured Darcy. What did he think of her? *STOP IT. He didn't, he was a... Relax*, she told herself. *Go for it, girl.* She owed it to herself. She slaved all week as a pharmacist's assistant and spent most weekends slobbed out with Scott in front of the TV.

"Miss Bennet," Darcy had said, "you must forgive my awkward way with words, which springs from hesitation on whether to compliment the grace of your deportment or the warmth of your smile."

Scott had never said anything like that to her.

"Babz," she said, running her finger round the rim of her glass, "you've role-played Elizabeth with Darcy before, haven't you?"

"Hey, you'll be fine. You'll soon learn to trigger his responses, just like I did."

That hadn't been what she had meant. "But, you've... been with him before."

"Don't worry, hon. Every encounter is wiped from their memory."

That hadn't been what she meant, either.

Babz etched a heart with her straw in her drink foam and winked. She was not only gorgeous, she was cooler than Kamila would ever be.

Stop putting yourself down, she thought. Tomorrow was to be the big day, climaxing in the Grand Ball. Champagne would flow (for the humans), proposals would be made after which guests and their partners were invited – encouraged – to make use of the wedding suites upstairs.

"Tell me, Babz," she said. "What are they... like?"

Her friend gave a low chuckle. "They're as good as you make them, hon."

*

Saturday morning went slowly. Darcy had been called for some unexpected business in London, or so it was announced. Kamila pictured him in the workshop, face flipped up, being retuned, but she hurriedly replaced that image with one of him on his horse cantering back to her, cape billowing in the wind behind him.

She spent most of the time sipping tea enduring Catherine Earnshaw droning on about her yeast-free diet. Thankfully Heathcliff turned up and took her out into the garden for croquet.

Across the conservatoire she caught sight of Babz sitting on Rochester's knee and putting her tongue in his ear. Rochester graciously smiled and offered the other one.

Kamila sat on the chaise longue by the French window, twirling her fingers round her reticule string. Her fingers itched to fiddle with her phone but she was sure Nevil's beady eye would be screwed onto the support room camera.

This really wasn't good enough. Where was Darcy? She'd saved up half of her holiday pay for this weekend. She blocked the thought and hummed 'God Save the

King'. She felt it was something Elizabeth Bennet would have liked.

"By yourself, Miss Bennet?"

Darcy loomed over her. His brow was moving slightly. She imagined the muscles moving in his arms.

"Er… yeah." Then inspiration stuck. "But I am never alone, Mr Darcy, with thoughts of you."

Woah, she thought.

"Solitude can greatly refresh one's appetite for company."

It was as if a tap inside Kamila had been turned on. "The anticipation depends on the quality of the company," she purred. "In your case, I am hungry indeed." Could she be discovering her inner regency belle? She snapped out her fan and lifted its floral pleats up to her eye.

"Come and join me, Mr Darcy," she said, patting the upholstery.

He sat down a couple of feet from her. "Am I too forward in saying that you have the freshness of the morning about you?"

She put the last vodka crème of the previous evening out of her mind and leant toward him.

There was a pulsation at the back of her throat. "Oh, Mr Darcy," she said. He leant over.

"Call me Fitzwilliam."

The name made her think of the men of the past: swords, horses, boot polish, velvet waistcoats, Macassar oil.

His mouth moved down toward hers. He smelt, strangely and alluringly, of cumin and plums. She closed her eyes in anticipation. Babz suddenly materialised in her mind, blowing vodka bubbles.

"Oh, Mr Darce… Fitz," she said, "Tell me, am I the

only one?"

"Why of course, my dear Elizabeth. I have saved myself for you."

"But what about the others? I mean... do you remember... or don't you? Oh, bugger."

A swarm of ants seemed to move under his brow.

"Please supply more exact parameters."

"Were you... did you...?"

"Unclear demand. Please retry."

"Let's forget it, shall we?"

"Please supply details of which files you wish to be deleted."

"Oh, please don't go la-la on me," said Kamila.

"Unclear demand. Please retry."

Where was Nevil? Her usual reflex took over when things were going out of control: she scrabbled for her phone.

As she pulled it out, Darcy's eyes swivelled a hundred and eighty degrees in their sockets, turning into small red eggs with dangling silver filaments. He snapped into a standing position. "Don't let your sword sleep in your hand," he roared.

A clot seemed to burst inside Kamila's brain.

"It's not a sword," she shouted, "it's only a machine. Just like you." She thrust the device at him, jabbing at it ferociously. "Look at it, tin man."

Darcy's face flew upwards to reveal the foam of sparkling lights.

The clot swamped her vision, her hearing and her thinking. "Gigabytes," she yelled. "Velcro. Elvis Presley."

His chest burst through his shirt. Wads of twinkling fibrous stuffing spilt out. He pulled Kamila into himself and marched up and down with her in a paso doble. A surprisingly tuneful sound rang from his chest.

"Won't you ple-e-e-e-ease…" He pushed the tangled nest which had been his face into hers as she froze rigid in horror. "Love me do-o."

"Hey up, Fitzy lad."

Mr Rochester approached, followed by a distraught Babz. "How are you doing, mate?"

Darcy let go of Kamila, who crumpled onto the floor. "We shall fight them on the beaches," he shouted.

Rochester cackled, shoved his hands into his pockets and whistled to himself.

Heathcliff rolled in from the garden, put his arm round Rochester's shoulder and they danced round the conservatoire kicking their legs and chanting, "*Olé olé. Olé olé.*"

Catherine Earnshaw and Queen Victoria appeared, their faces ashen.

Seconds later Nevil scurried in, frowning as he took in the scene.

"What's going on?" screamed Babz.

"They've turned random," he muttered. "And it's gone viral. Sorry." He approached Darcy with a screwdriver but the thing grabbed his hand and spun him round in a jive twirl.

Prince Albert goose-stepped in from the library. His sides had exploded. A silver rib stuck out, spongey matter dangling from it on strands of micro-wire.

"*Frohe weihnachten,*" he said and linked arms with Rochester and Heathcliff in their dance. Darcy stayed by the window doing physical jerks.

"*Olé,*" chanted Heathcliff.

"*Nurals schaffen da können wir vernichten,*" said Prince Albert.

"That is the question," said Darcy.

Rochester's left eye popped out like a cuckoo clock.

"I'll tell you what, boys," he said, "I'm well up for a bevvy. Time for the pub."

The robots all headed for the door.

"Do something, puffball," Babz yelled at Nevil who stared back at her with his mouth slightly open.

As Rochester went out, he glanced at the technician. "You joining us, mate?"

"You bet," said Nevil and they slouched, goose-stepped and star-jumped out of the room.

Babz dabbed furiously at her phone. It gave an ear-splitting whistle, which abruptly turned into the shipping forecast. It had gone random, too.

"Urghh." Babz's retort was like a squealing brake. Her arms flailing, she strode to a cabinet and pulled out a bottle which she angrily opened, took to the chesterfield and poured down her throat. "Gimme," said Queen Victoria, grabbing the bottle and taking a long draw. Catherine Earnshaw, surprisingly delicate, poured her drink into a fluted glass.

Kamila had not moved from her position on the floor, except once to put a rueful finger into the rent that had appeared in her silk dress. She pushed herself up, did a little hopping dance as she squeezed her slipper back on and strode out of the ballroom. Out in the foyer the receptionist sat frowning at a blank screen, frantically pressing buttons.

A hundred yards down the drive Kamila's phone began to work again. Scott appeared. He was mid-chew, a strand of instapasta dangling down his chin. It made him seem endearingly human.

"Fancy a change of plan, Scott? Why don't you come up here?"

The food muffled his reply but his eyes lit up.

"The conference has, er, disbanded early. But I've

still got the room. There's a four-poster bed..."

Maybe she could make something of the weekend after all. She shut her eyes and opened them again.

"And bring along a few beers as well."

It wasn't very Austenesque but what the hell. She'd stopped caring about all that.

~

Tony Kirwood's Biography

Tony Kirwood started taking his writing seriously when his sketches were broadcast on European TV comedy shows. He wrote material for Russ Abbott, *Shoot the Writers* on ITV, and for sketch shows, which he produced himself. He honed his gag writing skills with his short-lived stand-up comedy routine. He's written humorous and comedy-related articles for *Writers' News, The Independent, The Oldie*, and other publications, which flattered him by somehow finding his stuff funny.

His stories have appeared in *New Myths, Kzine* and at Story Fridays in Bath. He is currently writing a novel, which is an expanded version of a humorous column he wrote for his local newspaper. He inflicts his views on writing on the long-suffering students in his writing classes, while occasionally admitting he has as much to learn as they have. His book *How To Write Comedy* (Little, Brown) is a distillation of some of his teaching and was nominated for the Booker Prize for the most obvious title of the year.

As an actor he has appeared in numerous TV sitcoms. He was a Death Eater in the last two Harry Potter movies, though he likes to think he's actually quite nice.

SO YOU'VE BEEN CANCELLED

Shortlisted story, by George Riley

There was nothing quite like the thrill of the cancel.

Not that Oliver White believed in the term 'cancel'. Cancel was just the word bigots cried when they were called out; the whine of the right-wing predator as it succumbed to his moral lances. For Oliver, the internet was the great leveller – no longer could gloating celebs, tax-avoiding millionaires or populist ministers sail through life untouchable, corroding society with their toxic behaviour. Real people – *the* people – could now cut anyone down to size.

Oliver White. Journalist, author, socialist, feminist, anti-fascist. He/him. Rainbow flag. Green heart. Red rose. Black fist.

So read his Twitter bio. He had over 850,000 followers, though he knew many of them were tribal trolls, lurking there only to snap at his every post with crude slander or a homophobic jibe, decrying him and his supporters as the 'virtue signalling wokie army'.

"What's eating you tonight?" Max said, handing him a bowl with a wry smile.

Oliver looked up from his phone, frowning, as Max curled up in an armchair with his pasta and switched on the TV. "Professor at the University of Lincoln," he said. "He's reposted an article that claims certain tribes in Sub-Saharan Africa have lower intelligence. Doesn't look like his first foray into 'ethnic' science."

"Racist old white guy?"

Oliver swallowed a chunk of (organic, local cooperative) fusilli. "A racist old white guy in a position of power at a public institution, regularly invited onto the BBC, indoctrinating the next generation of young adults with his bigoted views."

"He's actually teaching them the racist studies?" Max raised an eyebrow.

"That's not the point." Oliver sighed. "The point is people have a right to know the vile ideologies of those in the establishment. I can draw attention to that. I can ask the university if that's really who they want representing them. It's not a crime to use the influence I have to call for progress. It's a moral obligation."

Oliver turned back to his phone. Firing off a perfectly barbed tweet was like pronging an arrow into the bullseye. But the real thrill came when the campaigns he was part of burst into the offline world. Getting blackface-normalising sketch shows dumped from iPlayer or an accused sex pest's memoir scrapped – that was satisfying. Oliver didn't enjoy when an academic got sacked or a disc jockey lost their slot on LBC – at least not on a personal level – but it was necessary for the greater good of society. That was the goal he always had to focus on. And these people were like knotweed; they always found somewhere else to spring up. No one was ever truly 'cancelled'. It had taken him five years to get Sadie Day banned from Twitter, and soon after she made a comeback on TikTok.

The right had become a hydra. The more you cut away at its insidious rhetoric, the more it erupted all around you. Oliver's inbox was bursting with messages from supporters directing him to the latest crime against morality. Nobody's reputation was immune to an unpleasant discovery, even cherished institutions and long dead artists. In the past few months he'd had to call out The National Sewing Society (ableism), Daniel Wilks (domestic abuse apologist) and even Dora the Explorer (racist). You could smell the fear in the air. Who would mark themselves for the cyber-guillotine next?

Oliver scoffed. "Have you seen this open letter, 'In Defence of Free Speech'?"

"No," Max said, disinterested, taking Oliver's bowl. "Are you gonna help wash up?"

"They act like they're the ones being attacked. As if a few comments on Twitter stop them pumping out their bile, which is *actually* killing people. Nothing says, 'I'm being silenced' like being paid to write about how you're being silenced in a national newspaper."

"Have I been silenced?"

"What?"

"I asked you to help wash up."

*

Oliver's allergies always started with a tingle under his tongue, spreading to a furriness around his throat, itching under his arms and inner thighs, before full blown hives, retching and throttled breathing. Being cancelled felt much the same.

First there was a Twitter mention, which he scanned in the microsecond it took to swipe away the notification on his phone: *Always knew Oliver White was an anti-Semite.*

He didn't think anything of it. Baseless smears went with his territory.

But then came the others. A trickle became a stream became a flood.

Absolutely heartbroken and FUMING #OliverWhite.

Liberal elite hypocrite shows his true Jew-hating colours #OliverWhitesOnly.

Guess that explains his Hitler youth haircut #WhitePower.

Oliver clicked. He scrolled. The same image cascaded before his eyes, over and over, one he hadn't seen in over a decade. Aged nineteen, first year of university, fresh-faced, arm round another boy – Anton – who was wearing a Julie Andrews wig and frock. Oliver was dressed as a German soldier.

"What the fuck?" he muttered. Just about to go down into a tube station, he pushed his way back through the grumbling flow of commuters. He put his (independent, indigenous women-empowering) coffee down on a wall and rushed out a tweet.

I am NOT and have NEVER BEEN an anti-Semite. I

have nothing but respect for the Jewish people.

Even before he could put his phone away, the barbed replies hooked in.

'The Jewish people.' Cringing so hard right now.

Bullshit. Bet you enjoyed being a Jew-fucking Nazi.

Oliver felt the air sucked out of his stomach like a punctured balloon. He had to get out of here. He had to get home. The thrum of people gushing down into the tube station filled him with a nauseous dread, so he stumbled away down the street, fingers shaking so much he almost ordered an UberPool by mistake.

In the taxi, he got more of the picture. Anton was now a dancer in Berlin; he'd mentioned the story of his partner wearing an SS uniform in passing, as part of a larger conversation about his time in England and his Jewish roots. He hadn't mentioned Oliver's name. But he had said how his partner had wanted to keep the outfit on when they had intercourse that evening. The interview had come out in a German newspaper a few days earlier. Web sleuths must have made the connection to Oliver and discovered the photograph.

He fired off another tweet.

The personal – and private – image that has been circulating was taken after my boyfriend at the time and I attended a Sound of Music singalong.

His phone dinged immediately.

Did you make him singalong to the German national anthem too?

Heat seared beneath his temples.

Hills are alive with the sound of Oliver White's bigotry #cancelled.

Always knew this guy wasn't kosher.

Jew hater.

Leftist scum.

He clasped the phone so tightly in his fist he was surprised it didn't crack. As they pulled up outside his flat, Oliver slammed the taxi door and stormed inside, forgetting to even give the driver a five-star rating.

Screeching along to an old movie doesn't give you the right to abuse minorities, you insensitive ghoul.

Proof the most woke are the most full of shit.

The latch shuddered in his grip as he closed the front door.

For the many not the Jew.

Pop. Oliver jumped. A cork bounced off the ceiling.

"Anniversary tipple?" Max grinned, proudly brandishing a bottle of champagne. He spotted the iPhone clenched in Oliver's hand. "I saw your name was trending too – double the reason to celebrate."

Oliver let out a frustrated sigh as he barged past Max. "And you didn't even bother to check *why* I was trending?"

"I assumed it was your latest article, no?"

Flinging his bag into the corner of the kitchen, Oliver was just about to offer a scathing reply when he found himself face-to-face with a man in chef's whites. He pivoted, scooting Max into a corner of the corridor with a questioning look.

"I booked caterers," Max whispered. "I told you. For our anniversary dinner."

"Shit."

"Why shit?"

"I have a Twitter mob to deal with tonight."

"Are you fucking real?"

"Yes, I'm fucking real."

Oliver gave him a kiss. It wasn't returned.

Calls for *The Guardian* to drop him. Petitions for universities to bar him. Old tweets resurrected –

criticisms of Israel, support for Corbyn – more 'proof' of his anti-Semitism. *Threads unravelled – This is the *real* problem with Oliver White – posturing* how his rallies to abolish billionaires were thinly veiled conspiracies against a perceived Jewish elite. *Just look how often he attacks Lord Sugar.*

The mob had risen up, hurling fistfuls of horseshit at Oliver, forming a giant pile of steaming excrement under which to suffocate him. He fought his way through the onslaught, posting rebuttals, scathingly critiquing the vilest replies. The ones that stung the most were those from the left, deserting him at the first whiff of imperfection. They'd repost his words as screenshots or discuss him as *Ol*ver Wh*te* to prevent him searching them out, as if his name were now a slur.

This is why we don't need privileged cis white men speaking up for us.

But occasionally he'd find a vote of support. *Dressing up for a musical is not a crime. Times change. Anti-fascists persecute Oliver White for dressing as a Nazi like… Nazis.*

He'd like each one, his thumb pounding on the heart icon like he was performing CPR.

The chef served them four courses at their kitchen table. Oliver barely ate a bite. "For God's sake," he muttered, "everyone goes as a Nazi for *The Sound of Music*. Anton never said anything about being uncomfortable at the time. We were teenagers for fuck's sake."

"But you did keep the uniform on when you had sex with him," Max replied, stony faced.

"I don't remember. We'd been partying." Oliver held his hands up. "There wasn't anything… it wasn't deliberate."

Max glared, then turned to the chef. "Thank you, Pierre. That was wonderful. The food, at least."

As he closed the front door, Max said he was going to bed. "You can sleep in the spare room," he added, when Oliver started to follow.

*

He hoped the rage would have subsided by morning. If anything, it had got worse.

One of the favourable tweets he'd liked had come from a notorious Holocaust-denying vlogger, which the mob had picked up on with delight. Pieces had been written up on the story on most of the news sites, with the *Mail* taking greatest pleasure in mauling Oliver as a racist hypocrite.

He swiftly reposted the article. *I have been called many things – communist, Marxist – but I will never be accused of being a racist. Those close to me, including my partner (who is Black), will tell you I have never uttered a racist word in my life.*

Still the bile continued to spew.

Here's why Oliver White's 'apology' is problematic.

He was prejudiced. Xenophobic. A bully. An abuser. Every attempt to fight back added fuel to the flames.

"Get your face out of that fucking phone."

Oliver snapped back to reality. It was evening. He hadn't noticed Max coming in through the door. And he'd never seen him this incensed.

"What's up?"

"What's up? I've asked you – I've told you – *explicitly* – not to talk about me online."

"I haven't, I didn't say anything about you."

Max held up his hands, flabbergasted. "You don't

even realise, do you? Christ almighty. Let me spell it out for you." He read from his own phone. "'My partner, *who is Black*'. Do you have any idea what it's like to be so casually dismissed like that? Do you have any fucking clue how hard I've worked to not be described as 'the black guy'? Of course you don't, you privileged white twat. You think a hard life is people saying some mean things about you on the internet. Well guess what, Olly, some people have mean things to deal with in the real fucking world."

"Uh..." Oliver was stunned. "I'm sorry, Max."

"Whatever. Just don't tweet a fucking apology."

"Wow." Oliver put down his phone, followed Max into the kitchen. "You think all I do is tweet?"

"I think everything you say is a fucking tweet. Every sentence you construct is a one-hundred-and-forty-character jibe, targeted to put someone down or assert your own moral authority. You're not interested in nuance or understanding anymore, you just like to snipe at the world from your virtual soapbox."

"Two hundred and eighty."

"What?"

"You can have two hundred and eighty characters on Twitter now," Oliver said.

"Jesus." Max grabbed himself a beer out of the fridge. "You want one?"

"Am I going to need one?"

Max shrugged and wandered into the lounge. Oliver poured himself a glass of (biodynamic, refugee-grown) wine.

"I didn't mean to demean you," Oliver said, taking a seat on the sofa opposite Max. "I just had to prove that I'm not the person they're trying to smear me as."

"And did you do that?"

"Uh… I… maybe. Some people are never going to accept it. We're in a war now, Max, like it or not. The right has mobilised and they're determined to obliterate anyone who tries to stand up to them."

Max rolled his eyes. "There you go again. You always have to blame someone else. It's the right, it's the billionaires, it's the Murdoch press, it's structural racism, it's society – it's never even slightly more complicated than that."

"That's because it's true. They want to keep people in the dark, but we're waking up. I want to *save* people."

"Is that what you're doing for me? Am I here to fulfil your white saviour fetish, Olly?"

"Fuck off."

Max sighed, fingers gripping the arms of his chair. "I admired you, Olly, you know I did. But that platform has warped your perspective. You think you'll genuinely change the world if your comments get enough likes and you post enough sharp quips. But that's not the way it works. You're burrowing into an echo chamber, closing your mind with every witty quote tweet… You've become the mirror image of the people you used to hate. And you're fuelling an even more extreme opposition."

Oliver felt his throat swelling. He took a glug of wine, unable to swallow the lump. "What are you saying?" he asked, not daring to look Max in the eye.

"It's over, Olly." Max's fingers released their grip on the armchair. "We're over. I don't want to be around whatever this is anymore."

Oliver begged. He pleaded. He called and messaged, till he found himself blocked. Cancelled. Alone in the flat, he opened up Twitter and posted.

Congrats to my so-called allies. You cost me my reputation, relationship, numerous speaking gigs and 5k followers. Way to set back our cause, never mind my personal pain. Maybe have some compassion and think before you tweet.

Oliver White settled back on the sofa, cricking his neck, rotating his wrist, ready to eviscerate the replies as they came in.

~

George Riley's Biography

George Riley likes to write about topics that he finds provocative or challenging. He particularly enjoys finding humour in the grind of daily life and the perils of his character's obsessive behaviours. Over the last few years, he has written many short stories – from the light-hearted to the downright horrifying – and has even published a collection of some of them. Alongside this he is continuing to work on a novel about a cult – a typically cheery subject matter.

THE TRUE STORY OF THE THREE MANBEAVERS

Shortlisted story, by Jonathan Sellars

I wrote a story once. It was called 'The Manbeaver'. I liked it. I liked it a lot. It had everything: drama, suspense, intense portraits of mother nature's fury, all topped off with a completely original I-never-saw-*that*-coming ending. I wish I could say that everyone liked it as much as I did but, thanks to the judges of the local

Russel Spout Literary Festival, I can't. And that's the truth. And the truth matters. Apparently.

The story was about a man called Rex Poteto. I called him Rex after my dentist. We'd always got on very well and he did a great job when I was unfortunate enough to lose both front teeth in a foolish ménage-a-trois between me, a night of heavy drinking and some concrete steps. You wouldn't have known my new teeth were false so, as a gesture of thanks, I promised to name a character after him in a story I had decided to write for the inaugural Russel Spout Short Story Award. I chose Poteto as my hero's surname because it sounds a bit like potato. It just makes you stop and think for a moment, doesn't it? My English teacher at school always said you know you've written something good if you can make the reader stop and think. She never specified whether that applies if all you're doing is making the reader stop and think of a vegetable. I think it does.

The premise of the story was this: One day, Rex goes out for a long walk deep in the wilderness. For hours and hours he clambers up over high ridges and down into deep, tree-filled valleys. Eventually, inevitably, day turns to night. But, as the sun starts to set, the sky does not fade to black like it should. No. Instead, red and orange begins to dominate the horizon. Rex's brow furrows. His palms dampen. Panic grips him. This can mean only one thing. Forest fire. Rex starts to run but it is too late. Before long he finds himself trapped between a wall of deadly flames and a raging river. Alas, our protagonist is doomed. But wait. Rex spots a family of beavers on the far bank and has a moment of inspiration. He drops to his knees and gnaws his way through the base of a nearby pine tree; he becomes a manbeaver. Soon the tree falls with a crashing thump, forming a bridge over the troubled water. Without a moment to spare, Rex crosses, destined to live another day, leaving behind nothing but the smell of singed hair and a few teeth. The End.

*

I arrived on awards day at the literary festival early, determined to get a good seat, one on the aisle, close to the stage. I knew 'The Manbeaver' would be like nothing the judges had ever read before and ran through my acceptance speech. Eventually the time came. But, as the winners were announced, I was left speechless. I didn't even receive as much as a mention, not even a tip of the hat or a, 'we loved it, but we loved a few others slightly more'. The judges could not have been clearer. They hated it.

I believe Kingsley Amis once said 'a bad review may spoil your breakfast, but you shouldn't allow it to spoil your lunch'. Well, Mr Amis, what happens when lunch is only provided for judges and competition winners and you didn't think to pack a sandwich just in case you didn't win? What happens then?

I sat there in silent rage. I even faced the ignominy of having to let one of the winners, Chris Fie-Something-Or-Other, shuffle past me to collect his prize. But, while Chris gave some nonsensical, rambling speech about 'how the way a story is told matters more than anything', I slowly regained my composure. I began to realise why my story had not won; there had been a mistake. I was not going to give up on my lunch just yet.

I retreated to the toilets to formulate a plan of action. As I searched for an empty cubicle, I happened upon the head judge, Dom Briccoli. Blocking his exit in the least threatening way possible, I casually enquired about my story. "It probably got lost accidentally. Don't worry though, I brought a copy with me. I can show it to you. Or I can tell you about it. Same thing really, isn't it?"

To my surprise, Briccoli was able to recollect 'The Manbeaver' just by the title alone, no synopsis required. "Oh, *that* one. Yes, we received *that* one." He looked just like Toad of Toad Hall. "But don't be ridiculous. We want this to be a serious event. It's not for works of fantasy."

"Fantasy?" I cried. "It was a completely original story. It was no more fantasy than any other work of fiction ever written."

He rolled his eyes the way flat-earthers do when you tell them that the world is round. "A man biting through a tree? Really? I mean, who's ever heard of something so stu—" Perhaps at that moment my body language became a smidgen less un-threatening. "So unimaginable."

"But that's what good fiction is," I screamed, quietly. "Imagining something that no one's ever imagined before and bringing it to life, expanding the frontiers of the reader's imagination. If it's happened before then it's not fiction."

"My boy." He laughed like a toad as well. "I am afraid you have it all wrong. Good writing, good fiction, is not about making things up, it is about truth. It is about being believable." His hands gestured like he was wrapping some elaborate gift. It was incredibly irritating. "A great story should take the world around us, make sense of it, and turn it into something comprehensible for a reader to enjoy."

"But that's just a history textbook. All you're doing is taking something that's already happened and repackaging it as your own."

"Well..." He smirked. "I'm afraid we shall just have to agree to disagree. I have a lunch to attend." With that, he pushed past with unnecessary force, causing me to set off the hand dryer. As he reached the toilet doorway he turned. I couldn't catch much of what he said due to the loud buzzing in my ear but, whatever it was, he looked incredibly smug as he said it. All I did hear was "...enter next year's event. Who knows, perhaps you might have written something more believable by then."

As the door swung shut I shouted after him, a little desperately perhaps, "Did it at least make you think of a potato?" He did not respond.

I bought a soggy sandwich from a shop on the way home. Then I sulked for the rest of the day.

*

About six months later, something rather unbelievable happened to me. You might have actually read about it in the news, I occasionally get asked for interviews even now. I'm always happy to give a brief overview of the key details along these lines:

Like an oil tanker near rocks, I can sometimes be reckless in bad weather. Ever since I can remember I've always loved being outside in storms. I don't know what it is about the lashing rain, the booming thunder and the bolts of lightning ripping across the sky, but I find it impossible to just sit inside and let them pass.

That afternoon, I happened to be taking a stroll by the river when a fierce storm blew in. Rather than heading up to high ground or shelter, I headed down to the river's edge. I took great pleasure in watching how the pounding rain distorted the water's surface, mesmerised by nature's power to turn something so placid and slow-moving into an angry torrent in a matter of minutes.

For a fair while I stood there in blissful ignorance, unaware that not only was there nobody else around, but that the river was also beginning to burst its banks. By the time I did become aware, it was too late. The slightly raised patch of bank that I stood on was now an island with a population of two; me and a tall, thin alder tree.

Lightning flashed. Thunder roared. Fear engulfed me.

The river continued to rise and I knew there was only going to be one resolution to my predicament: drowning. My fate sealed, I slumped down onto the soggy ground, my back resting against the alder tree, and, I'm not ashamed to say, started to sob.

But then, suddenly, most unexpectedly, something struck me. Lightning. No, I joke (I know it's a cruel joke but I always enjoy the way the interviewer gasps). That would have absolutely marmalised me. It was an idea; an idea struck me. Rex Poteto, my story. I dropped to my knees and started chewing frantically at the foot of my island companion. I chewed that alder tree like a ravenous beaver, hoping with all hope that when it fell, if it fell, it would be long enough to reach the high ground nearby.

And it was.

I was found by a journalist from the local paper. By chance, her dog had been spooked by the storm and run down to the river in its disorientated state to where

I lay slumped on the grass, cold and exhausted, having crawled to safety across the makeshift bridge. I was missing some teeth and was highly distressed but had no other visible damage.

The journalist took me to her house to warm up. I proceeded to tell her what had happened and after a quick conversation with her editor I made the front page the next day. The rest, as they say, is history.

I always end any interview by showing the picture that the journalist took of me the next day, smiling goofily next to the fallen tree, teeth in hand. The story of the tree-chomping man was picked up by several national papers and, like I said, you may well have come across it. For a short time, a very short time, I enjoyed what I would call D-list celebrity status. I appeared on numerous local radio and TV programmes and even got to meet professional adventurer Bear Grylls who described my ordeal as 'truly unbelievable'.

I also wrote up the event in a story and, after careful consideration, I decided to name it 'The Manbeaver' (a second manbeaver story). And, like the first manbeaver, I thought it was competition worthy.

*

I have to admit that the food options at the second Russel Spout Short Story Award winners' lunch were a little disappointing. Too many vegetables, too little meat. The prosecco was free though and there was certainly enough of that to go around. I was slightly worried about meeting Dom Briccoli again, but I needn't have been. He was all smiles, a real picture of charm, and I assumed he had in all likelihood forgotten our heated discussion the year before. The other judges and winners were equally charming, constantly coming over to me to compliment my story. For that magical fifty-seven minutes my D-list celebrity status returned. "And can you believe it?" I could hear them say to each other, "That actually happened to him, 'The Manbeaver' is a *true* story. I saw it in the news. How incredible."

Just as I was leaving, Briccoli took me to one side. "You see," he said, "what did I tell you last year?" His face was thick with self-righteousness – he *had* remembered. "Fiction has to be rooted in truth. It just has to be. Can't you see I was right now? Your story won this year because I could believe it. Because I knew it could happen. Because it felt so *real*." I nodded, allowing him to bask in his self-anointed glory. "And isn't it remarkable," he added, "that you wrote a story about a trapped man biting down a tree last year and then, *quelle horreur*, it only goes and actually happens to you? You couldn't make it up. Doesn't the world work in funny and mysterious ways?"

"Yes, it does." I smiled. "Yes, it does."

*

Would you believe that the winners of the third Russell Spout Short Story Award are announced tomorrow? You might be surprised to discover that, not only have I entered again, but my entrance is once more called 'The Manbeaver'. That's three now.

As with the first manbeaver story, I have used Rex Poteto for the name of the protagonist. I could have used my own name, but I didn't. This time the story starts with Rex having an argument with a toad-like literary judge called Tom Cauliflyer. Rex is unhappy because his story about a man who bites down a tree is discarded for being unrealistic and pure fantasy. Rex argues that a completely original story, one that requires complete imagination, should be much better rewarded than a story based on something that has already happened. Cauliflyer disagrees. Cauliflyer says that he could only ever believe and enjoy a story if he knew that the events in it were possible, if they had already occurred in real-life. After a long sulk and a soggy sandwich, Rex vows that he will prove Cauliflyer wrong. A few weeks later, Rex goes out for a stroll during a storm. He happens upon a fallen tree that has formed a bridge to a small island. Rex has an idea. He makes two phone calls. The first to his dentist to discuss the possibility of having some fake teeth removed and to ask whether he could keep a secret. The second to a heavily disillusioned friend who works on the news desk at the local gazette. Over the next few months, Rex goes to the river whenever a storm breaks out. Eventually, he gets lucky; he finds another tree-bridge. Rex puts his plan into action and is able to trick the whole country (including Bear Grylls) into believing that he gnawed down the tree like a beaver in order to escape certain death. Rex, however, is not finished. He then writes a story about this fictional tree-gnawing, enters it into the same writing competition as the previous year, and delights as he enjoys wonderful reviews, a winner's trophy, and a slightly disappointing free lunch. Rex takes particular satisfaction when Tom Cauliflyer commends him for writing a story rooted in truth. Rex wonders the best way to reveal to Cauliflyer that the whole thing was in fact completely made up. The End.

I'll find out tomorrow what Dom Briccoli thinks of the third manbeaver story. I like it. In fact, I like it a lot.

In theory he should too. After all, unlike the first two, apart from the names, it's all true. But I'll be bringing my own lunch. Just in case.

~

Jonathan Sellars' Biography

You won't know who Jonathan is. You probably don't care who he is either. But, if you do ever stumble across him (and his photo won't help with that as he doesn't usually make that facial expression) he's a pretty nice guy who writes a lot with not a lot of success. He thinks the lack of success is because nice guys tend to finish last but, deep down, he knows that it's because not-great-writers also tend to finish towards the back of the pack. Maybe his day will come, maybe it won't.

He has two children, neither of whom can read or write. He's not worried about that. Yet.

He also lies on Instagram: @jonathansellarslieshere

VADER

Shortlisted story, by Todd Sherman

I'm slowly falling apart.

There's a ringing in my ear. Inexplicably. All of a sudden.

My shoulder hurts. Probably because of my knee.

My back hurts. I'd weed-whacked earlier and, later than never, my lats are screaming for submission. I don't have a strap for the apparatus. I just wanted the lawn mown – clean cut – out of sight, out of unbodied mind.

That goddamn ringing in my ear.

Twenty-three minutes into Spanish black metal and my leg started to sink into sand that had once been concrete. Stopped. Stretched. Ran again. Pain. Sinking. Stop again. Stretch again. Start. Pain. Stop. Pain. Limp until a friend passing in a car beeps and pulls over.

I know I put in earplugs for that metal show days ago, so why is my ear still ringing? Someone left a phone off the hook in my head. Wired. Dumb. Unable to surf the net or vet anything I may've said or let me go to sleep, goddamn you, let me drift into ringless peace.

Adrift. That was the name of that Spanish metal band. Man, I'd really been hauling ass, too. The best run I'd had this season. While I was talking to my friend through his car window, a man stepped off his porch with a bottle of iced water that was far more ice than water. I put it to my knee with thanks. My friend drove away. I limped off. I waved to that man back on his porch. The ice melted enough for me to drink it by the time I'd gotten home. I'd run quite a way.

When I push myself up from the couch, I wince. My shoulder. My back. My fucking knee.

At least I'd started running again. A lot, considering the damage. Three days a week. Over fifty minutes per session. I'd never felt so old and useless. Some guy with a dog on a leash had run past me. Jesus Christ with a four-and-a-half-inch nail in his pes anserine bursa.

Darth Vader must've always been in pain. Always had a headache, right? Maybe that's the real reason he went to the dark side. All that buzzing pain, that incessant thumpthumpthump, those itches in places that couldn't be scratched for all the plastic, the gear, the apparatuses that maybe made his lungs itch with each dark-sided intake of air.

All cyborgs must hurt. Especially where the meat meets the non-meat in an uneasy truce at the junctions, the joints, the aching knees. Fuck, those plastic and metal and meat bodies have got to be heavy.

Darth Vader must've been heavy as shit.

Not as heavy as that Spanish band when I'd been lugging my less-heavy body down the sidewalk at black metal speed.

Now I'm limping like only an old man can limp during the healing phase that may not be a phase but more properly a permanent state of motion, an unending condition of bartering the things that I can't do anymore for the things that I'd never cared to do in the able-bodied past.

I'm not going to jump over the thing.

I'm not going to try and catch up to that dude jogging with his dog.

I'm not going to get that six-pack back unless I cut down on the beer, since I can no longer run off the fat.

But now I can get to writing that six to eight-hundred-page short story collection I'd put off three books ago.

Maybe now I'm ready to tackle *Finnegans Wake*.

I've got more time for tending the garden with the wife.

Darth Vader didn't even need that lightsaber. All affectation. He could move shit with his mind.

Maybe when I break down enough, become fully cyborg, fully half of what I once was, I'll be able to move shit with my mind too. In the future. In a galaxy not-so-far away.

For now, I'll have to play metal and rock out on the click clack couch. Wince as I get up. Curse my knee, yet bless my burgeoning powers of telekinesis and metacognition.

Vader fader later gator.

Could I even outrun an alligator if one stumbled out

of the woods? Can an alligator even stumble with such stubby legs? We don't live too far from the river. Not too far from the swamp. Maybe snapping jaws would greet the wife and me in the backyard, somewhere next to the thrusting necks of the ghost pepper plants.

I'd need that lightsaber. It wouldn't be mere affectation.

Later, gator. I'm a fading Vader.

Standing hurts. Sitting hurts. Bent knee. Propped up on the coffee table. A long pillow between the legs. The warm bone and flesh beneath the kneecap.

Darth Vader must've always been hot. All those fused intersections. A liquid-cooled suit, surely. Ready for battle. Saber in hand. Fingers flexed on the other hand and pointing still at the rebel he'd thrown against the wall with his mind.

Mind alone.

Mind over matter.

All that matter burns like miniature suns all over what's left of the mortal within the plastic suit.

I'd flattened the lingual cusps of my molars so badly that I keep biting my tongue. Really rip that fucking muscle open and bloom a battlefield in my mouth. At least a lightsaber would cauterise the wounds.

All that clenching. Black metal. Doom metal. Weightlifting. Running and running. Unremembered dreams. Nightmares, maybe. The *Dark Star* always sucking at the artery in the neck that never stops vomiting blood.

Existence is an endless war.

Constant bartering.

What you can't do. What you hadn't considered could be done, now accomplished. Fucking toss that lightsaber to the *Death Star's* deck and throw all those bastards to the walls, to unforgiving space with the force of will and will alone.

Not alone.

Someone helps me tend the garden.

Or maybe I'm helping her.

Maybe she's breaking down, too.

Vader to Vader.

Except she can't stand black metal. Hates to run. Never bites her tongue. Doesn't lift heavy weight over her head in repetitions with no other purpose than lifting that weight again and again.

Strengthening muscles that'll only atrophy over time.

Crushing teeth that won't be able to crush solid food.

Pavement ground into quicksand.

A ringing in the ear that matches the wail of black metal.

Falling apart sucks, man.

I'm a man of motion, not a couch-grown potato.

I grow chili peppers that momentarily blind the mind with their heat. Their sting. The white light from clipping the tongue and the river of blood to follow.

That alligator will have to learn to swim and roll and stumble its stubby legs in blood.

Bloody ghost peppers.

Hold my hand, wife. Hold me, but don't squeeze too hard. My shoulder still hurts. My back. My knee.

Thank God it's raining. I don't have to weed-whack the lawn.

Thank God it's Saturday. I don't have to go to work.

Thank God for another week of heavy metal heavy bodies heavy cyborgs fucking heavy humans on the bed lying sideways since standing up and pounding hurts too goddamn much.

Blood on the *Death Star's* decks.

Blood on the face of the *Dark Star*.

Hold me and don't let go, wife.

We'll tend the garden with our minds.

Maybe remember our separate dreams upon waking and share those dreams with each other and decide to return to blissful rest.

If Darth Vader had had a long pillow between his legs – if he'd had someone to spoon in a dark corner of an Imperial Star Destroyer – if he'd traded his lightsaber for ghost peppers – maybe he'd not have needed to choke out underlings with his mind, or explode planets, or get in a death duel with his son.

Poor, poor Vader.

Sympathy for the devil.

Cry me a bloody river.

Bite your tongue, bite the red light of the saber, bite down and crush your teeth, bite at the vacuum of space once you'd been mind-booted out the ship's bay. Bite down on this and tell me if it's worth chewing anymore.

I think I'll choke down a couple of ibuprofens.

Foam roll the legs.

Eat a sandwich with pepper relish and drink too many beers.

Start buying large T-shirts instead of mediums.

All part of the bartering system. All part of the new state. The new permanent phase, until even permanence becomes as impermanent as the cartilage between bones of very heavy, ever-slowing, truly ringing mortal beings.

I think I'll ice the knee and sit and think and think for a while.

I've got a telekinetic will to nurse.

A superhuman desire to become more and more as I inevitably become less and less. Physically. Finally. Forever. Into neverness.

Goddamnit, though, I was really flying to that song before the knee went to mud.

What a badass tune.

I can still hear the ringing.

~

Todd Sherman's Biography

Todd Sherman is alive in Wilmington, NC. He is an author of novels and short stories, or so we have it on good authority. And that authority has been granted by the angels – even if those angels have long since fallen to earth. So we surmise he writes by demon-power and may not realise it. Is, in fact, blissfully unaware that he even exists. But he breathes, we can swear it. His stitched-together host body crashes through this world.

Todd Sherman is the express property of Klaxon Corp.

www.amazon.com/Todd-Sherman/e/B00O57573Y

WHAT HAPPENED

Shortlisted story, by Edward Field

"What happened?"

"What *happened*?"

"WHAT. HAPPENED? Hmm?"

"Ummm. What happened was..."

"Yes?"

"Um. *Chris* happened."

She flicked through the notebook with her not-very-hairy, shiny thumb stump and saw me watching. "Constabulary standard issue."

"Half a thumb is standard issue for a cop?"

I'm not good with understanding faces – *happy, sad, I want to stamp on your head* – those faces. *Facial expressions* they call them, but they all look pretty much like the same face to me. My social worker told me afterwards the face she gave me was probably *incredulity*, otherwise known as *What the fuck?* I've drawn it from memory in my book of lists in the *Faces* section. I think I'll remember that one in future, which makes five now.

"The notebook."

"What?"

"*Pardon.*"

"I said, 'What?'"

"I heard. You said '*What?*'"

"I know. I just told *you* that."

"Yes, but it's more polite to say 'pardon'."

"Oh."

"My *notebook* is standard issue. My half a thumb isn't. It's just a lasting reminder of my only summer as a postal worker. You should remember that."

She's right. I should. But I have problems remembering things that aren't important, and you can't tell me somebody else's half a thumb being eaten by a shih tzu – it's a kind of dog; I looked it up – half-crazed on crystal meth the babysitter dropped under the sofa the night before is more important than remembering the *What the fuck?* face. I can't remember *everything*. My brain is just the average one thousand, three hundred cubic centimetres which, though pretty impressive, is still a finite space in which to store memories I've created, everything I've learnt, and instructions on how to operate the over 650 muscles, 206 bones and five vital organs (and almost one hundred non-vital organs) in my body. I have to be selective, and with 7.6 billion people on this planet (rounded up to the nearest hundred million), that's roughly 15.2 billion thumbs. I've given it a great deal of thought, and I really do think it's more important that I remember a few more faces than the current whereabouts of 30.4 billion thumb *halves*.

And that's exactly what I told her.

She gave me a different face that didn't match any I've got on my list, though it was closer to *constipated* – I drew that one from my face in the mirror when I'd been trying to have a poo for thirty-six-and-almost-a-half minutes but still couldn't get more than a Coco Pop out – than it was to *happy*.

Her thumb stump found the note she was looking for in her constabulary standard issue notebook. I think I might steal it when she isn't looking. The notebook, not her stump.

"Chris the plumber?"

"No. Drummer. I don't think she's good enough to plumb. She's not really good enough to drum, either. She keeps missing. Are you allowed to be a plumber if you're only thirteen?"

"No. I don't think so. So... Chris. Not *Christopher*?"

"No. Christine."

"*Christine*?"

"Yes. Christine. It was Christine who chopped my leg off with the chainsaw. *That's* what happened."

"That was *Chris*?"

"Yes. But she didn't mean to."

"Oh?"

"She was aiming for my neck."

"She's not very good with her aim, is she?"

"She's not very good at lots of things. Hang on, I've been making a list."

"Don't worry about that now, Sara," – that's my name. Sorry, I should've told you earlier, I s'pose – "I'm more interested in what happened."

"But that *did* happen."

"Before."

"No. That happened *after*."

"Yes. I know Christine chopped your leg off after. I'm asking what happened before."

"Before before? Or just before?"

"Is there a difference?"

"Duh."

"Please don't be rude to me, Sara. I'm not in the mood. Jim left me yesterday and he accidentally took my car keys – at least, I hope it was accidentally – and I can't find my spare keys so I had to catch the bus to the police station and then walk here, it was late, it's raining, I'm soaked and I haven't even had breakfast. And he emptied our bank account."

"I didn't like him."

"Neither did I, actually. I think that might be why he left me."

"Not because you did the sex with Mum?"

"No. That might have been part of it, but he was a very angry man."

"One happened before the other."

"You're right. You can be very perceptive sometimes, Sara. I think maybe he was angry *before* I did the sex with your mum."

"I mean *before* happened just in front of Chris chopping my leg off with the chainsaw. *Before before* happened before *before*. Earlier."

"Oh. Right. Of course."

"Who did you think chopped my leg off?"

"What?"

"*Pardon.*"

"I said— Ah, yes. Sorry. I meant who do you think *I* think chopped your leg off with the chainsaw."

"I don't know. I'm not very good at knowing what other people are thinking, but you sounded surprised when I said Chris did it."

"I was. I am."

"So was she. I think I was more surprised though. Hmm. *No.*"

"No?"

"No. *You're* surprised. She was *more* surprised and I was *most* surprised she chopped my leg off with the chainsaw."

"Right. Thank you, Sara."

"You're welcome. It's a good job her aim is bad, isn't it? Otherwise you'd be talking to my neck stump now."

"I'm not sure I'd be talking to you at all."

"Why? Are you stumpist?"

"What?"

"*Pardon.*"

"Yes."

"You are?"

"Are what?"

"Stumpist. It's not very fair. I know my neck stump would be bigger than your thumb stump, but there's no reason to be jealous. Are you jealous of my leg stump, too?"

"Sara, I'm not jealous of you at all – I love you – but—"

"Does that mean we have to do the sex?"

"Wha— *Pardon*? No. Only Zena— Mum— *Your*

mum... Only your mum and I do the sex."

"All over the world?"

"No. Just the bedroom. And the kitchen sometimes. And—"

"I mean you and Mum are the only people all over the world who do the sex?"

"No. Of course not. I just mean I don't want to do the sex with you. I never will. Ever."

"Because my stump is bigger than yours?"

"*No*, Sara. Because you're only thirteen, and I love you differently than I love your mum and if we can work everything out, then you'll be my stepdaughter."

"So, it's a good thing, then?"

"What is?"

"That Jim left you."

"Yes."

I find adults very confusing sometimes. They're older and are supposed to be cleverer than me, but I haven't met a single one who can keep up with me yet. My thinking, I mean. It's like when Yolanda – oh, that's her name: Yolanda, stumpy thumb cop who does the sex with Mum and might be my other mum one day (I wonder if that will make her Mum-two or Mum-too. *As well*, I mean.) – like when she had her baby, Simeon. He isn't a baby anymore. He's just a boy and annoying. But when he was a baby, he was so scrumptious I said I wanted him inside me and Mum and Yolanda thought I meant I was going to eat him, but who eats babies? I was only eight then and I wouldn't have been able to finish a whole arm, even if I *did* want to eat him, which I didn't. But he was so cuddly and giggly and he made my tummy jump up and down and all my insides do the wiggly things and I wanted to cuddle him with my whole body so that nobody could ever hurt him and I could feel the wiggly things in my insides forever. And they really thought I was going to eat him. Adults are well weird.

"And you really don't mind that my stump is bigger than yours, Yolanda?"

"Of course not. And don't let them hear you call me that."

She said that with the face that I think is *happy*, but it had a wobble in the mouth.

"Why? Isn't it really your name? Does Mum know?"

"No, silly. I'm just not supposed to be talking to you as your, um, well, almost other mum. I'm meant to be talking to you as a police officer, trying to find out what happened."

"But I keep telling you. Chris chopped my leg off with the chainsaw when she was aiming for my neck."

"Why?"

"Why what?"

"Why...? Hold on, let me get this straight. *Before* – not *before before*; we'll deal with that in a minute – just *before*. Before she chopped your leg off with the chainsaw, why did Chris want to chop your head off?"

"She didn't."

"I know she *didn't* – I can see it. I'm talking to it – I mean why did she *want* to chop your head off?"

"She didn't. She was just pretending to chop my head off, but the chainsaw is very heavy, and she isn't very good at aiming – even when we throw stones at Mister Unsworth's greenhouse—"

"I didn't hear that."

"I said EVEN WHEN WE THROW STONES AT MISTER—"

"Yes, thank you very much, Sara. I think the whole hospital heard that time. I'm just going to pretend I *didn't* because I'm being a police officer at the moment, not your almost other mum, remember?"

"Oh. OK."

"Let's go back a bit."

"To before?"

"I think so. The bit that happened in front of Christine pretending to chop your head off?"

"When Chris picked up the chainsaw and switched it on?"

"Yes, that's good. So why did Christine have a chainsaw and why did she switch it on?"

"To chop the wood."

"What wood?"

"From the sideboard."

"There was wood in the sideboard?"

"No. *I* was in the sideboard. The wood *was* the sideboard."

"Why were you in the sideboard?"

"I was not being Penn."

"You've always not been a pen. Why would being in a sideboard change that?"

"Not *a* pen. Penn. I wanted to be Penn for once, but Chris beat me at rock, paper, scissors with her nuclear explosion joker, so I had to climb inside the sideboard and be Teller again."

"What's a pen and teller?"

"*Who.*"

"Who's who?"

"Penn and Teller."

"What?"

"*Pardon.*"

"Sorry. Yes. So Penn and Teller are...?"

"Whos."

"Whose what?"

"*Pardon*."

"No—"

"Yes. You said it was rude when *I* said '*what*'."

"It is, Sara, but that's not what I mean this time. What I'm trying to understand is Penn and Teller."

"Are."

"Pardon?"

"Well done. And it's 'are', not 'is' because they're 'whos', not 'whats', because they're people not things."

"And they were there with you?"

"I wish. If they had been, Chris might not have chopped my leg off with a chainsaw. Why are you eating your hand, Yolanda?"

"I'm trying not to scream, Sara. I'm also struggling to understand what happened."

"It's not hard, Yolanda. We were playing Penn and Teller again – they're our favourite magicians and one day we're going to Las Vegas to see them – and I lost rock, paper, scissors to Chris's nuclear explosion, so I had to climb into the sideboard and be Teller and she stayed outside and was Penn, but we didn't have a chop saw so she used a chainsaw."

"To try to chop off your head?"

"No. To *pretend* to chop off my head."

"But why?"

"Because most magicians saw the lady in half—"

"Which lady?"

"All of them. But it's boring and that's why Penn and Teller use a chop saw and why we used a chainsaw and Chris pretended to chop off my head. Maybe that's why Jim left?"

"You think Jim left because Christine pretended to chop off your head with a chainsaw?"

"No. Because he wasn't angry; he was bored."

I think that was when Yolanda covered her face with her hands and made strange noises. They sounded a bit like the noises she makes when she and Mum do the sex, but as Mum wasn't there and Yolanda won't do the sex with me, maybe she was just pretending to be a seal. It wasn't a very good impression, but Mum says it's not nice to tell someone they're rubbish at something they're trying to do. What you have to do is be *diplomatic*. I haven't learnt that face yet and I won't lie to anyone, so I tried to be nice and gave her a round of applause.

The first thing Yolanda did was take her hands away from her face. The second thing she did was make a face that looks quite a lot like the *I've got diarrhoea and I've got to hold it in* face. I wasn't sure if she wanted another round of applause, so I changed the subject.

"Can I have my leg back?"

"Oh God, please help me. No, Sara, you can't have your leg back. Didn't they tell you? They can't sew it back on."

"Eurgh. Good. That'd be gross. Why would they do that?"

"They can for some people."

"Not for you and your thumb."

"No. But the shih tzu swallowed it."

"And when I pick my boggies, I don't put them back again, do I? That would be grosser. I eat them instead."

"You want to *eat* your leg?"

"No. I want to paint it pink and keep it on my bookcase."

"Why?"

"It's my favourite colour."

"I mean why do you want to put your leg on your bookcase?"

"I don't think it will look right on my chest of drawers."

"Sara—"

"OK. Fine then. I don't want my leg anymore. You can have it."

"*I don't want your bloody*— And breathe. One. Two. Three—"

"Do you need help, Yolanda?"

"Probably."

"OK. Four. Five—"

"Not with counting, Sara. I'm going to try this once more. See if you can give me a simple answer. What happened to Christine?"

"Before *before* or after?"

"*Now.*"

"She's in the freezer."

I don't know what Yolanda was trying to do, but her scream hurt my ears a very lot and when she shouted the *What the fuck?* words, she was wearing totally the wrong face. Maybe that's why Jim left: Because she was sending him mixed messages.

Yolanda didn't even kiss me goodbye this time. She just wandered out of the ward pretending to be a zombie and said, "I give up," to the nurse who was wrapping up my stump. I didn't know we were playing a game. If she'd told me, I would have tried harder.

Adults can be really hard work sometimes. And if I'm being honest, I think Yolanda was a little bit rude walking out like that. I hadn't even got to the best part: What happened before *before* Christine chopped my leg off with the chainsaw.

~

Edward Field's Biography

Edward Field is a writer, editor and the author of *Permission to Rage: The Book on How to Complain Effectively*, as well as three children's plays currently on the South African curriculum. He writes and edits fiction, non-fiction, scripts, speeches, corporate presentations & brochures and his work has appeared in anthologies, websites and publications including *The Stage, Breathe, Reflex Fiction, 101 Words, Storgy, To Hull And Back* and *Idle Ink*.

Website: www.squircle.me
Twitter: @EdwardSquircle

WHEN YOU LEAST EXPECT IT

Shortlisted story, by Navaris Darson

Friday

"Did you hear about Emerson? He found $20,000 in a bathroom stall at Panera Bread."

"Didn't he just get a $20,000 hiring bonus?"

"Practically a month apart."

I'm catching up with my friend, Ricky, at a boutique café and patisserie in Beverly Hills. He proceeds to explain how Emerson took the money to the police, and if no one claims it in a week, he'll get to keep it. But I'm only half-listening.

At the age of 44, I still haven't won, inherited, or accidentally stumbled into $20,000. Which is quite uncommon. Especially at my age. Pretty much everyone I know has received twenty-grand by now. At *least* once.

When the bill arrives, I offer to split it, but Ricky won't hear of it. Ricky and I once worked together as valets at Chateau Marmont. Then five years ago on New Year's Eve, he received a $20,000 tip from Matthew McConaughey, because Matthew 'dug his vibe'. Ricky took the money and gambled it all on crystal energy bracelets that he now sells from a designer van outside of Erewhon at double the cost.

Ricky does well for himself.

Before we part ways, Ricky asks me how I'm making money these days.

I tell him I've been doing simulated patient work at UCLA. I don't tell him that I only make $20 an hour and that, earlier in the day, I was 'presenting signs of severe rectal prolapse'.

We hug goodbye, and he throws me a green bracelet. Jade. Tells me it'll attract money.

Then he says, "Hang in there. It'll happen."

Sure, sure.

Saturday

My friend, Shannon, and I meet for a walk at the park across from her apartment. She's an artist in her late 30s, and she hasn't received $20,000 yet either. We met while singing in a gospel choir in college, and I like Shannon, because she knows 'de struggle I's seen' and she knows 'de sorrow'.

As I seethe at the unfairness of Emerson's good fortune, she doesn't minimise how I feel. She doesn't offer me dime-store clichés like: *Don't look for it. You'll win $20,000 when you least expect it.* She just listens and holds a space for my emptiness. I extend the same courtesy when she confides she's depressed about turning 40 next week. Like me, she really thought she'd have gotten twenty G's by now. As we walk, she dejectedly scans the park for cats in the desperate hope of receiving a lavish reward for returning one to a neighbour.

I know that sinking feeling. A week before my 40th birthday, I pulled up the floorboards of my apartment on a hunch. All I found was dust and mouse pellets. The Universe might not always provide, but it definitely disappoints.

My heart goes out to Shannon. She's one of my best friends. Would I trade her friendship for twenty-large? In a heartbeat. The beautiful thing about our relationship is that she knows that, and I know she'd do the same. We keep it real.

Still, I wish I could help somehow – throw her a $20,000 bone, you know? If only.

At night, I read a chapter from *The Power of Dow* that asserts there's $20,000 inside each of us at all times. We just have to 'invest in ourselves'. Tell that to my landlord when the rent is due and I try to pay with imaginary inner money.

I open the drawer of my nightstand. It's full of small, black Moleskines that I use as manifestation journals. I grab the most recent one and flip to the first blank page to try a new 55 x 5 manifestation technique I found on Instagram.

I write 'I'm grateful for winning twenty-thousand smackers' 55 times. Then I put my journal away. One day down. Four more to go.

Before falling asleep, I Google 'abundance crystals' from my iPhone.

Sunday

I call my mum and we talk for an hour. You'd think The Universe would slip a smooth twenty-thou to a fella who phones his mum once a week, but not so much.

She hears the sadness in my voice, and she understands to a small degree. She didn't get her $20,000 until she was 29, later than most. For a long time, we didn't talk about it because she and my dad are devout believers of the Written Cheque. Growing up, we had a bronze statue that hung in the foyer, an exact replica of Ed McMahon, his head raised to heaven and his arms stretched wide, bearing a giant cheque from American Family Publishers. A reminder, that Ed paid the ultimate price, so we might yet win.

When I was 20, I came out to my folks – told them I was interested in computer transactions and preferred direct deposit. I was terrified. They said they still loved me then strongly advised me to keep it to myself. Months later, my mum called me when I was back at college and told me I broke my dad's heart that night. I hung up the phone and sobbed.

Now, before our call ends, she makes me chant, "Show me the money," with her from *Jerry Maguire*, and then she tells me that she and my dad pray every day that I'll get a nice direct deposit for twenty-grand soon. My eyes well up. It's not what I really want: it's not twenty-thousand big ones, but they love me for me, and it's something.

Later that night, while scrolling through Facebook, I see that my friend, Tobey, is out of the hospital. He dressed up as Scrooge McDuck for Halloween and suffered a neck injury from diving into a Jacuzzi filled with two kilos worth of coins. I love Tobey, but seriously, he gets twenty-grand, and I don't?

I mean, it's not like I'm not putting myself out there. I'm on all the sweepstakes apps. Sweepstakes Lovers, Give-a-Way Frenzy, even Sweepr (though I refuse to send nudes). I've even won a little bit here and there. Small change. $2,000. Nothing to write home about.

Emerson texts me: 'Did you hear the news?'

I don't text him back.

Monday

During my morning session, my therapist reminds me that the best way to receive is to be happy for others when they receive.

Ugh. Fine. I call Emerson to congratulate him.

"Hey, man. Another 20K. So wild."

"I know, can you believe it?"

I can. He's still waiting to see if anyone will claim it, but I doubt anyone will. His life is just that charmed.

Last year, Emerson held an investment ceremony after his third $20,000 windfall. After blowing through $40,000, he was finally ready to commit his money to a Roth IRA account.

I had just won $10 on a $5 California scratcher.

It was a big week for both of us.

After the ceremony, I stood in a cluster with all those 'yet-to-receive' as Emerson prepared to throw a bouquet of origami one-dollar roses over his shoulder.

Supposedly, whoever caught the bouquet would be next in line to get 20K. But I'd already caught six bouquets by then, and I'd grown sceptical of the claim.

Not that I needed to worry. Emerson's cousin, Lisa, sprang like a python and snagged it before the rest of us. Within weeks, a bus slammed into her 2005 Kia Sorento. A month later, guess who wheel-chaired out of the courthouse with a $70,000 settlement and a brand-new Chevrolet Volt. Not me.

I swear, some people have all the luck.

Tuesday

An hour ago, I was stretched out on a hospital bed at UCLA exhibiting symptoms of a simulated subdural hematoma as a doctor-in-training told me my prognosis was fatal. I *wish*.

I'm in the lobby now, waiting to collect my $40 payment. A kindly older woman turns to me and tells me her grand-daughter just won the grand prize in a bikini mud-wrestling contest. She beams with pride, then asks me how I got my first $20,000.

I get that assumption often.

On first glance, you'd never know I've never been the recipient of a lump sum payment of twenty-thousand simoleons. I'm conventionally handsome. Intelligent. Funny. And kind. *Charitable*, even. The kind of guy you'd think people would want to give money to.

Around 6pm, I get a text from my dad: 'New singing competition show. $20,000 prize. Worth a shot? [Basketball emoji]'

But we both know I don't have any skills impressive enough for reality television. I can't sing. Or bake fancy cakes. Or design clothes out of junkyard scraps. And

Lord knows I've tried.

I text him that I'll look into it (a lie), and then I ask him about grandpa who had a bad tumble in September, morbidly curious about the possibility of a sizeable inheritance on the horizon. Dad informs me that he's better: '92 and as strong as an [ox emoji]'

Figures.

Wednesday

I just finished writing 'I'm grateful for winning twenty-thousand smackers' in my manifestation journal. 55 times a day for 5 days. I close the little black notebook and return it to my nightstand.

I'm waiting for tonight's winning lotto numbers to be posted.

On my left wrist, I'm wearing five different crystal abundance bracelets (thanks to Amazon Prime's two-day delivery). I've also got a 528Hz 'Receive Unexpected Money' frequency playing from YouTube, and for extra measure, I've anointed my lottery ticket with a dab of manifestation oil that I purchased from a mystic I follow on Twitter.

Tonight's the night *it happens*. I can feel it.

I close my eyes to visualise what I would do if – no – *when* I win $20,000 in the lottery tonight. A lot of people blow through their twenty-grand quickly. They buy a pontoon or fritter it all away on tropical vacations. I'd be smart. Like Ricky. I plan to invest mine in real estate and flip it for a small fortune. I've waited a long time for twenty-grand, and maybe I'm old-fashioned, but when it comes, I want it to last a lifetime.

I get a notification that the numbers are in. *It's happening.*

I scan the lotto ticket with my phone, and I see the message:

'Sorry. This ticket is not a winner.'

My ticket is eligible for the Second Chance drawing, but the prize for that is a pittance of $15,000. I don't even bother.

I slide off the bracelets and toss them into the trash.

I always hope, and it's the hoping that hurts the most.

I really believed tonight was the night.

I really needed it to be.

Thursday

A horrible thought occurred to me last night: *What if I claimed the money?*

The idea was clearly unethical (and possibly illegal), but also… seemingly fool-proof. How would the cops know it isn't mine? Plus, it's not like Emerson *needs* another $20,000. And in a way, I'd just be balancing the cosmic scale.

By morning, I'd made up my mind.

Now, my car idles across the street from the police station and I'm shaking. I can't believe I'm about to do this. As I open the door of my car, it's as if I leave my body, and I watch myself cross traffic and walk up the steps of the station. I get all the way to the glass doors, and then… I can't. As desperate as I am for a double stack, I can't get it like this. Fie upon my damnable conscience.

Moments later, back in my car with my head pressed to the steering wheel, I get a text from Shannon. She's received an unexpected $20,000 art grant from a mysterious benefactor. Days before her birthday.

And now it's just me.

I feel the tears form as I look up at the orange-pink sky through my windshield, and then I think, *Good for Shannon. She deserves it.*

And I mean it with all my heart.

I take one look back at the police station, and then I start up my car to head home, knowing that the hard choice is the right choice and certain that this is what it feels like to have twenty-grand inside.

~

Navaris Darson's Biography

Navaris Darson is an actor, improviser, singer and writer who lives in Los Angeles, California. As a writer, Navaris enjoys writing poetry, personal essays and short stories. In the past year, he has written a short comedy play, completed over seventy-five poems, and co-written two different TV sitcom pilots.

Outside of writing, Navaris teaches improv and guest-performs at The Groundlings Theatre and School. In addition to acting in television shows (including *2 Broke Girls*, *The Other Two*, and *American Horror Story*), he also appeared on the 85th Academy Awards with the Gay Men's Chorus of Los Angeles, and he's sung with choruses at Disney Concert Hall, The Hollywood Bowl, and Carnegie Hall.

For more information, you can check out his website: www.navarisdarson.com. Plus, he can be easily found and followed on Instagram, Twitter and YouTube. Believe it or not, there aren't a lot of Navarises out there.

WREN BALDWIN'S THANK YOU-O-METER

Shortlisted story, by Rob Widdicombe

When Wren Baldwin's wife Audrey told him he had to clean out the garage and look for items to sell at their upcoming yard sale, he instantly got a rock in his stomach. Wren Baldwin looked out the window at some clouds and said to himself, "Oh, no."

Then she said if we don't make at least $300, Jenkins can't go to summer camp.

"But," Wren Baldwin said.

"But what?"

"Not the Thank You-O-Meter."

"That thing?" she scoffed. "No one's gonna buy that anyway."

Wren Baldwin was off to a slow start in the garage. The years of random junk tossing had made a devastating mountain. The Thank You-O-Meter was in there. Wren Baldwin knew where. It was generally in the far corner, underneath Mount Clutter.

Where it was safe.

"The Thank You-O-Meter isn't for sale," Wren Baldwin randomly told Audrey again later in their kitchen. "This is for certain."

She looked away and whispered, "*Jesus. Fricking. Christ.*"

Out in the garage, Wren Baldwin had a price tagging gun that he had bought for $39.99 at Staples. He would pick up a rusty pair of grass clippers, or a creaky old floor lamp, or her tuba, and then examine it, turn it over, cock one eye, estimate its value, tag it and set it on the yard sale pile. But not the Thank You-O-Meter, which was to remain hidden under a smaller junk pile in the corner.

After a few hours of sorting, he was down to one big mound of trash, a large assortment of 'maybes' and one medium pile of what he estimated to be about $7,500 in yard sale merchandise. Wren Baldwin put the items for sale out in the yard and then sat down in the garage on a lawn chair in front of where the Thank You-O-Meter was. He waited for the yard sale to begin.

"You're not done yet?" Audrey yelled, storming into the garage, approaching the small pile that was hiding the Thank You-O-Meter. "Anything of value in here?"

She began rummaging.

"That's just... nothing," Wren Baldwin said.

"What about these cat headphones?"

"Please, don't," he said, now alternately pacing and squirm-standing.

"Wait, oh Wren. You're seriously hiding this 'thank you' thing here? My god, you are *losing* it." She took the cat headphones and left the garage. Wren Baldwin then rearranged the small clutter pile to further obfuscate the Thank You-O-Meter.

The garage sale wasn't going well. By 3pm they had only made $241. As things were winding down, Wren Baldwin's wife popped into the garage and said, "A couple of quirky freaks are out here buying the Branson riverboat gambler hat. I bet they might buy the 'thank you' machine. Let's get it out, come on."

"It's my Thank You-O-Meter and it's not for—"

"We've got to do it for Jenkins," Audrey insisted, pushing him out of the way and quickly digging out the Thank You-O-Meter.

"No," Wren Baldwin yelled as she zapped out of the garage with his cherished gem. Paralysed with anxiety, he began pushing his temples together with his palms and holding his breath. Then he looked out front and, sure enough, the bearded ironic bros had purchased the Thank You-O-Meter and were already putting it in their car. An incredible blast of energy and will then rose forth from the rock in Wren Baldwin's stomach, turning it into a stunning power blossom of righteous action and he ran out of the garage and through the yard sale and up to their car, shouting, "Hey, hey."

The two men were already in the car and about to leave when they were startled by Wren Baldwin's screams.

"Hey, guys," Wren Baldwin screamed, flopping awkwardly across the hood of their car. "I just want to say thank you. Thank you so much. Many thanks. Really appreciate it. Can't thank you enough. Thanks again. *Thank you.*"

Wren Baldwin got his footing and was coming around to the passenger window to thank them again when the two men drove off as fast as they could without saying anything.

Wren Baldwin sat down on the front lawn, exhausted. The yard sale was over. Only he and his wife were there. Jenkins was in the back yard doing his mayonnaise project.

"What the hell was all that yelling?" Audrey asked.

"I just wanted to make sure I got a good score in case they had the Thank You-O-Meter turned on."

"Well, we made $317 in total, so we're all good for camp." Audrey beamed.

"I hope I got a high score."

"Great job, Wren."

"It was one of my better *thank yous*."

"No, I meant great job getting stuff ready for the yard sale. Come on, let's clean up."

Wren Baldwin stretched out on his front lawn and started falling asleep. He remembered back to the time when he was a small boy and his father had given him the Thank You-O-Meter.

"Now as your pledge to me," his dad said, "you must keep this forever. Unless you ever need to, like, sell it to take care of your family or something. Well, son... what do you say? Son? What do you say?"

"Oh," young Wren Baldwin said, "um... thanks, Dad."

Then the Thank You-O-Meter made an aggressive buzzing noise. "Darn it all, Wren," his dad snapped, deeply disappointed. "You only got a 3."

Wren Baldwin knew that selling the Thank You-O-Meter was the right thing to do. The summer camp where they were sending Jenkins was expensive, but it was the only one in the area that was willing to give him his ankle massages. Wren Baldwin then gently fell into a blissfully contented lawn nap, his mind cascading softly into an inescapable dream of being chained to a steaming radiator while thousands of terrified field mice sang the *Love Poems of Richard M. Nixon* into a small hole in his forehead.

Thank you. Thank you so much. Many thanks. Thanks again. Thanks.

~

Rob Widdicombe's Biography

Rob Widdicombe was born in Virginia, USA, and is still alive. He enjoys staring out of the window and thinking about space chickens, generally speaking.

JUDGES' STORIES

BIGGER ON THE INSIDE

Judge's story, by Mike Scott Thomson

I want to regenerate.

I want to throw back my arms, puff out my chest, look straight upwards to the infinite beyond, and let my whole body explode in a violent burst of nervous energy. Then, when I'm done, I will be a new man. Ready to face the universe again. Ready to once more travel forward in time.

Upstairs, the colour of the carpet marks the place of the bed we once shared. Faded squares on the wallpaper reveal where our pictures used to hang. Only one remains: there's you, my faithful companion, veiled and radiant in white, beaming to the camera. And then there's me, with my dark tweed suit and question mark waistcoat, and a stick of celery in my lapel instead of the traditional carnation, and a fedora on my head, and an ancient glint in my eye. Two people, looking forward to adventures in time and space.

Alien and mysterious; that's who I wanted to be. That's how I wanted you to want me. But I guess you eventually saw through that. Saw me for who I really am. I have only one heart, so I suppose that makes me human. Now this one heart won't stop hurting.

The last removal man's just left. I asked him to leave just one chair. So he left the kitchen stool. There's one exactly like it from the TV movie, near where the Eye of Harmony opens, so it will slot in perfectly. I carry it across to the den. This room, it's not large; not like it is on the telly. There's a miniature console in the middle, and circular patterns on the walls like in the classic era, and some old levers and buttons I got from the scrapyard. If the Time Vortex could distort the hours I spent working on it, giving those hours a spatial equivalent, it really would be bigger on the inside.

I put the stool down and leave the room. The rest of our house – my newly empty house – gapes in front of me. Without you here, it's vast. It's huger than the human mind can possibly comprehend. This is the real fourth dimension, and I am a centuries-old renegade, lost within, destined to be forever alone.

I want to go back to how I was, when we first met. When all that was, all that ever could be, was a beguiling myriad of possibilities. When I was the real lord of time, and all the time I had, I gave to you.

I want to regenerate to a previous version of myself. But I can't, because that wouldn't be canon.

~

Mike Scott Thomson's Biography

Mike Scott Thomson is a writer of fictions of different shapes, sizes and styles – one day he should probably make up his mind. A few good places have published his work over the years, including anthologies from the Fiction Desk, Momaya Press, Bridge House and National Flash Fiction Day, and literary magazines such as *Litro*, *Prole* and *Storgy*. That's also his face riding The Hog on Chris Fielden's first ever To Hull And Back collection, way back in 2014.

Mike is also responsible, in cahoots with the esteemed Mr Fielden, for encouraging the literary community to wantonly overuse that much-maligned linguistic tool: the adverb. Several hundred published stories later, there now exist five anthologies in aid of the literary charity First Story, with a sixth on its way.

Website: www.mikescottthomson.com

Twitter: @michaelsthomson

~

Mike's Competition Judging Comments

Goodness me. This never gets any easier.

At the risk of once again sounding like a stuck record (and being responsible for the wanton use of literary clichés), the quality of writing and storytelling has been outstanding. Judging these tales to belong in any sort of 'order' has been nigh-on impossible. But, that's the job of a judge. Where does one start...

In previous years where I have assisted with this competition, I usually do have a clear winner. Not so this year. For me, ten stories – that's exactly half the shortlist – could have easily made my podium positions. And out of this top ten, four of them could have been my overall winner. I have never had to be so picky, finicky and, frankly, judgmental, in my life to get anywhere near separating them out.

I doubt, of course, that my results are anywhere near what my esteemed judges have decided for themselves. But that of course is by design, not accident, and the overall results will make fascinating reading. At the time of writing, I have no idea who's won, but from what I've read, it will be well-deserved. Whoever it turns out to be: enjoy your moment.

LOVE ISLAND – THE EVICTION

Judge's story, by Mark Rutterford

It's a slow day. A cold day and things are somewhat... wrinkled.

Some days are like that: exacerbated by the season, the jet stream and boxer shorts.

Cotton, cool, boxers. Perfect for the summer but a bit breezy at this time of year.

We endure and we wait. My friends and me. We're patient, saving our energy for better days, warmer days, when things are somewhat more... strident.

We wait, in an orderly fashion, trying not to be impatient, trying not to write to the papers about the overcrowding. The overcrowding is getting worse. You hear that, don't you. Public transport, prisons, cities, countries – the whole planet. Our world is Earth-like... well, it's round anyway. And it's getting busier.

As a community, we're very sensitive to issues of climate change. It's a bit like trying to get your nan and grandad out of the house – there's a prescribed and specific set of optimum conditions (still, dry, sunny but not too sunny, 71.4 degrees, larks ascending etc.). It's a bit like that for us. We're obsessed about it, if I'm honest – we're like Greta Thunberg and David Attenborough on acid.

That's another trait of ours, the population of our world – we're hyperactive. There's a lot of energy, a lot of activity and jostling. It makes for a full-on existence and I'm ashamed to say, we're a bit shallow, somewhat one-dimensional... superficial. It's like all of us, in our world, are on TV. *Big Brother, Strictly, Britain's Got Talent*, you know the score. Desperate to be noticed, desperate to stand out, desperate to be picked, to get the vote, to be chosen. *Love Island* – that's basically where we live... who we are.

Did I mention the over-crowding? It's getting worse, seems like it's getting worse by the day. It is a problem, there is friction and discontent and you have to stand up for yourself to survive. I wish I had some elbow room but then... I wish I had elbows. Anyway, *Love Island* with serious overcrowding is the scenario and it's no laughing matter because there's a shocking mortality rate as a result. Millions of us, in cramped and sometimes intolerable conditions, all hustling to survive.

No wonder religion is so big here. Deliverance is the thing, we all want deliverance – it's literally an escapist theology. We don't do gods like you do gods – Buddha, Jesus, Tom Hardy. We're not ones for the stand-out saviour as such. It's more aspirational than that.

Our spiritual journey has some similarities to those in your world. We have a nirvana – a Heaven, if you like. We endure, we strive and our journey is long and tiring – we must not falter, we must keep going for at the end of our quest, we will be free. No more hostility, no more dissatisfaction – fulfilment in a place of peace, harmony and growth. We're big on personal growth.

Freedom's nice, but our goal is more personal than that and there's more to our spiritual enlightenment. We travel on, happily and with boundless energy, hoping that we might be chosen, for to be chosen is what we want more than anything. More than all the other *Love Island* contestants, more than the narcissistic Ronaldo, more than Trump, Putin and Lukashenko, more than the Kardashians, more than writers submitting to magazines, competitions and literary agents, hey, more than the Apple corporation itself... we want to be THE ONE.

We have a version of Hell too. We have many versions of Hell and they keep us awake at night with worry. Imagine living your whole life committed to escape, freedom and deliverance. You know the odds are stacked against you because there can only be one that is THE ONE amongst millions. But there is hope that The National Lottery big finger of fate might be pointing in your direction and maybe, just maybe 'it could be you'.

Hang on, is something happening? There's just a hint

that maybe today could be a special day. Something in the breeze? Maybe it's just hormones. Ignore me.

Hell takes many forms in our theology. The dry and barren cloud in which nothing can thrive – in which we are crushed and discarded. It's always a white cloud for reasons I don't quite understand. Then there is the escape that flounders on fortifications that cannot be breached. Unnatural barriers, marketed as defences against deliverance when the reality, I have to say, is closer to genocide. There are fairy-tales about failures of quality control that result in the rubbery defences falling apart, but which of us believes in such fortune – good at that? There are chemical weapons in Hell, all trying to destroy us, and then – and this is the most upsetting of all – there is the void. The unknown, the nothing, the place that isn't a place but in which our journey ends and we die. Spillage.

There it is again. Something is stirring. I'll apologise now but I may have to go.

Hell's a bit scary, I think you'll agree. I know it's meant to be scary, I know it's tough out there, but if you're a sperm – a sperm like me, whose very existence is based on escape and deliverance and being chosen – you just wish there were more versions of Heaven and fewer versions of Hell.

Whilst I'd love to stop and chat, I can't hang about. That something in the breeze has turned out to be an air-raid siren and there is going to be an escape tonight. Sometimes these things are over very quickly, you may have heard that too. To be honest, if it gets me to Heaven I don't care.

I'm ready, I've always been ready, I could be THE ONE.

This is my chance, I'm starting my journey... wish me

luck.

You could at least wave.

Here we go...

~

Mark Rutterford's Biography

Mark Rutterford writes and performs his short stories in towns and cities across South West England, quite often with a prop in hand. Stories with a love interest, a bit of humour and a slice of heartache. If you see him, tell Mark you like his big heart and he will love you forever.

A proud member of Stokes Croft Writers, Mark is looking forward to regular meet-ups in the future and the return of Talking Tales whenever and wherever it happens. Whenever and wherever there is an opportunity to tell a story, that's where you might find Mark. He'll be casting a big shadow, eating a biscuit and waving... or wearing... a prop.

Website: www.markrutterford.com

Twitter: @writingsett

Facebook: www.facebook.com/MarkRutterfordWrites

~

Mark's Competition Judging Comments

You know some writing competitions tease you with an article from a judge about what they're looking for? It's good to have an insight but it's a bit like chasing last week's rainbow and a long since emptied pot of gold.

Here's what I'm looking for.

A story – a finished story, although not everything has to be neat and tidy or fully explained.

Humour – in some form and I'm not particular about belly laughs or wry smiles, humour is a broad church.

Fairy dust – I know that's a little hard to pinpoint, but that's the point. The fairy dust could be a character, a voice, use of language, rhythm, a plot twist or a unique and brilliant idea. It could be one, all or none of these things… like tomorrow's rainbow, you'll love it when you see it.

There was lots of fairy dust in a brilliant shortlist that was lots of fun to read.

Congratulations to everyone in the anthology and thank you for your stories, your humour and your unique and brilliant ideas.

PROBABILITY GREEN'S RETORTING SPIDDLE

Judge's story, by Alan MacGlas

The eighteenth century saw some remarkable mechanical inventions in Britain, helping to give the country a critical lead in the agricultural and industrial revolutions that multiplied the profits already accruing from the slave trade, thereby enabling her first to resist and finally to defeat Napoleon's bid for hegemony in Europe and establishing her as a world power for one hundred and thirty-seven years. Notable examples of these machines included Jethro Tull's horse-drawn hoe and seed drill, Hargreaves's spinning jenny and

Arkwright's water-driven looms, along with less specific but no less important developments in refining, smelting and manufacturing processes pioneered by such giants of the age as Wilkinson, Hunt, Wedgwood and the Darbys. It was the dawn of the great age of mechanical engineering, which was to see wood replaced by coal, stone by steel, horse-power by steam-power, and eventually the internal combustion engine and rocketry. (I can't off-hand think of anything that horses did that has been replaced by rockets, but the statement stands.)

Some of those great machines from that early industrial age can still be found in a few preserved and prized museum pieces. They are usually objects of considerable size and naked construction, the kind that we find increasingly rare in our world of electronic miniaturisation and streamlining. But very few originals survive. The Bolton Museum contains the sole remaining working model of Samuel Crompton's spinning mule, and its famous predecessor, Hargreaves's jenny, can now be found only in illustrations or reconstructions.

On the other hand, there are, here and there, pieces of mechanical engineering which have outlived their industry and survive as mysterious relics, undiscovered by curators of our industrial heritage and uncollected by those weird people whom one sees buying and selling stuff on television auction programmes. Such a machine is one that I shall now describe to you.

I met it in a wine-bar converted from an old wharf-cellar beneath London Bridge on the Southwark side, the area which in medieval times had been occupied by a neighbourhood of stews, taverns and gaming houses owned by the Bishop of Winchester. It squatted in a broad nook against the cellar wall in the candlelight, serving as nothing more than a source of idle conjecture for the clientele of City workers when they ran out of things to say about money over their bottles of Antipodean claret.

The machine was massive, weighing at least a ton, made chiefly of cast-iron, with fittings of lathed steel, brass, wood and leather. It sat on wheels of iron, of the flat-rim kind that used to be fitted on trucks in mines or quarries where the flange was put on the rail instead of the wheel. Upon the chassis was set a labyrinthine construction of parts worked by various rods, levers, cogs and cylinders. It was more or less balanced, but the two sides were not symmetrical; and it had a front and a back, though which was which was not immediately apparent. There was a leather seat for the operator, positioned to put him or her in control of what appeared to be the machine's essential device, a large and immensely powerful screw-socket. Add the details that the ensemble was mostly black with age, apart from the yellow brass plates, brown yew handles and a few red patches of rust, and the description is complete – apart from one small detail: nobody had the faintest idea what it was, or what it did.

Abhorring a rational vacuum as much as nature abhors a physical one, I undertook my own research: and thus am able to bring to you one of the Industrial Revolution's most idiosyncratic technological triumphs and commercial failures: Thomas 'Probability' Green's Retorting Spiddle.

Primitive spiddles had been used since ancient times for the scarrowing of raw thrax, a time-consuming process necessary to get rid of impurities and tease the dactylic fibres. Though arduous, this labour brought considerable rewards: the detritus obtained from scarrowing was valued by ancient civilizations as an element of wattle-and-daub, and the Romans also added it to wine as a mellowing agent and preservative for long distance transports (it was probably less toxic than lead, which they used for similar purpose). The industry left cultural traces as well: the name 'Rumpelstiltskin' originated among medieval thrax workers in the Black Forest, inspired by the thud of the cresping truncheons and the workers' elevated wooden pattens, which they wore to avoid the wash of the urine on the stone floor, and to discourage Swiss brigands, who prized Bavarian calfskin boots.

In England, the production of thrax was concentrated in the Three Choirs counties, where timber, charcoal, iron and incest were all readily available in the Forest of Dean. The crespers and scarrowers of Hereford and Worcester refined the prime thrax and separated out the various products for the merchants and shippers of Gloucester and Bristol. Even today the Ross-on-Wye coat of arms depicts a coroneted helmet overgrown by the luxuriant green hair typical of women who worked with thrax for a decade or more.

This last point is pertinent: scarrowing was generally seen as women's work, while their menfolk were engaged elsewhere in agriculture and crime. Industrial historians have likened it to the production of tweed in Scotland or poultry-rearing in southern and eastern England, which were also traditional crafts undertaken by women while their menfolk were abroad fighting, reciting poetry or fornicating with livestock. For this reason, the introduction of Probability Green's spiddle did not provoke the Luddite attacks that affected weaving and other male-dominated industries. In any case, Green's original spiddle was a relatively simple machine which, whilst obliging the cresper and scarrower to work in tandem, kept both of them in employment, provided neither of them was taller than five-foot-three.

Thomas Green had been born with four elder sisters to Prudence Green, a granddaughter of Sir Weonard Napier of Puncknowle in Dorset, who turned pirate, went on a four-year voyage of terror and rapine, returned with his plunder and sat for twenty years as a magistrate and Member of Parliament for Bridport. Prudence, who had been widowed before any of her children were born, owned a successful brewery and brothel in Dorchester in consort with the highwayman Jack 'The Dragon' Drago. Thomas acquired the name Probability from his baptism: when Drago, as his putative Godfather, was asked if he forswore the Devil and all his works, he answered, "Probably." The Green Dragon brewery was later sold to Charles Eldridge, whose wife Sarah was an entrepreneurial powerhouse; together they founded the famous Eldridge Pope brewery, which some readers may recall as Dorchester's most distinctive commercial landmark until early in the twenty-first century, when it was demolished to make room for expensive cramped apartments, boutiques, coffee-shops and other facilities essential to modern life. But none of this is relevant.

Young Thomas proved to be a gifted mathematician and draftsman. He was fascinated by the rudimentary machines he saw in his mother's property and neighbouring workshops, observed the smiths and millers of Dorchester at their business, and visited Bridport to learn the secrets of rope making and real tennis. He became notorious for suggesting new mechanical solutions to increase efficiency or reduce costs, until at last the local bigwigs ran out of patience and ordered him to "desist these wilful, vexatious and French improvements."

Frustrated, he joined the Navy, in which he served for nine years, rising to the rank of bosun's mate. Sailing vessels of those times provided excellent tuition in many necessary skills and principles of design, which stood him in good stead when he lost a foot off the Azores, resigned his warrant and returned to live in Lyme Regis, a town where matching legs conferred no advantage in getting up and down the steep spume-blown streets.

Supported by a share of his family's beer and brothel profits, Green occupied himself once again in study of mechanical crafts. It took him only a few months to devise his first spiddle, popularly known as the 'Marry-Me' because of the potentially immodest position of the operators astride the shaft. But his greatest achievement, the retorting spiddle, took a decade of trial and error to develop. It was a radical advance: not only did it combine the dual crafts of cresping and scarrowing, but it also incorporated the tertiary process of rasputing, enabling a single machine to subsume the labour of several dozen manual workers and dwarves.

If Green could have produced this machine fifty years before he was born, it would have made his fortune. Thrax had been in high demand throughout the eighteenth century as British merchant ships penetrated all parts of the navigable globe apart from Antarctica (then known as Hellman's Land from its whiteness) and the North American Back Passage, which continued to defy explorers for another century.

Not the least of thrax's value was to the Navy itself, providing *inter alia* a vital waterproofing ingredient of the pitch used in caulking, a savoury sauce for boiled haddock and a prophylactic against the pox. In 1757 when Admiral Byng was court-martialled and shot on the quarterdeck of HMS Monarch as an encouragement to other admirals, thrax was so important to the Royal Navy that a codicil to the Thirty-Seventh Article of War decreed execution by hanging at the yardarm for any member of the crew who "doth adulterate or abandon the goodly store and provision of thrax, to the endangerment of His Majesty's vessel and impediment of His Majesty's purposes."

Unfortunately, the retorting spiddle came to a market in which the cold light of day was approaching its twilight. The expansion of imperial bounds enabled by the might of British maritime power and its attendant commercial success proved to be the thorn in the ointment for thrax: the discovery and exploitation of masidue, a much cheaper rival product readily available in the New World, undercut the market for thrax in much the same way that the discovery of crude oil undercut the whaling industry, in spite of the superior quality and versatility of the elder product. Once the Flemish scientist Hugh Janus had isolated the essential ingredients in masidue and realised that the peptides and neaptides could be broken down by the washing process invented by Sir Benjamin Washing, removing the need for constant supplies of fresh urine, the writing was on the door for thrax as a profitable commodity.

The total number of retorting spiddles ever made is not known, but it was probably less than seventeen. Commercially naïve as he was, Probability Green never took out a patent on his invention. The tragedy of this was that his retorting mechanism anticipated at least two potential patents which could have secured his family's fortunes for generations. The more obvious of these was the dromedary gears which governed the feeding of the thrax to the frame for rasputing; but even more revolutionary was the design of the cylinders which injected the phosphate of pangolin necessary for high-speed scarrowing, powered by a threnody of the detritus in a design not seen again until the development of jet engine after-burners in the later part of the twentieth century.

Both thrax and masidue were overtaken by synthetic products after the First World War, thanks to the German genius for Ersatz, so most people alive today have little knowledge of them, whereas quite a lot of them have heard of rhubarb, which the Germans promoted as a substitute for lemons. Incidentally, thrax is known as 'Hornsand' in Germany, from the two German words *Horn*, which means horn in English, and *Sand*, which means sand. This coinage was necessary because, notwithstanding that the root word *thraxa* is Anglo-Saxon, modern Germans are always uncomfortable with dental fricatives. But this was of no help to Probability Green, who did not speak German, and had been dead for many years.

The thrax industry left no dramatic traces on the landscape such as those bequeathed by mining and forestry. Evidence of its existence in Britain – apart from the solitary splendid machine in the London Bridge wine-bar – can now be found only in such traces as the Ross-on-Wye escutcheon, the occasional revival of the name 'Crispin', the preservation of skills in charcoal-burning and incest in the Forest of Dean, and the city of

Gloucester's annual gift of a cough-lozenge to the reigning British monarch, in memory of William IV, the so-called Sailor King, who was overtaken by a paroxysm in a cresping-shed where he and Mrs Jordan had taken shelter from sudden rain and the prying eyes of an impudent populace.

For those who wish to view the relic spiddle *in situ*, London Bridge underground station can be reached on the Jubilee Line and the eastern branch of the Northern Line. However, I cannot guarantee that the machine or indeed the wine-bar itself is still there, as it is at least twenty years since my visit. Also, I'd partaken what we Scots call a 'sensible modicum' of a house beverage at the time of my observation, and my recollections may be coloured as a result. Look, I'm doing this for free. If you have any complaints, take them up with Christopher Fielden, and while you're at it, ask him where the money really goes.

~

Alan MacGlas's Biography

Alan MacGlas, a Glaswegian born and educated in London, is a retired government servant and current professional editor of stories and poetry. He won the 2019 To Hull And Back short story competition.

~

Alan's Competition Judging Comments

Reading a collection of solicited short stories sent in from many corners of the English-speaking world is always a stimulating experience. The creative spark may produce diamonds or it may produce a clinker: as a long-time editor of prose and poetry, I anticipate both. Polished literary skills are useful but not essential to a writer; good ideas, intelligent plotting and sheer enthusiasm are more likely to get an editor's interest than elegant but vapid style. The one unforgivable crime is to bore the reader. I am happy to confirm that none of these stories bored me. On the contrary, it's evident that the To Hull And Back competition is going from strength to strength in its encouragement of new writing, and new writers. If I have one disappointment, it's that the quotient of real laugh-out-loud humour across these selected stories is spread a little thin. But that isn't surprising, even in a competition devoted to humorous stories, because – as any top comedian will confirm – humour is in fact one of the most difficult genres to master, and all the more credit is due to those writers who achieve any success in it, which includes all the authors in this book.

UNWELCOME GUEST

Judge's story, by Lynda Nash

The groom's family were a rambunctious lot, squashed shoulder to shoulder around a trestle table, while we sat like four tent pegs, trying to fill the empty space between us by spreading our arms until our elbows met, and talking over each other.

There were more dinner courses than us, so we invented another sibling. Lanky like me but he had my brother's cowlick, my mother's cheekbones and the expression my father keeps in a tobacco tin for match days. His pock-free skin shone under the strip light and his teeth were Colgate-white. His name was Colin or Cameron or Troy – we couldn't agree. I had wanted a sister. Someone I could have mani-pedis with and watch *Love Island*.

Having recently been promoted to managing director, our new brother chatted amiably about office politics and told sartorial jokes about the government, which we didn't get. He could programme computers, name the constellations and sing like Justin Timberlake. His wage was salaried and his ISAs capped. Cambridge University had given him an honorary doctorate in biodiversity, he raced part-time for Ferrari, and bought his supermodel wife a speedboat for their first anniversary. My mother was disappointed not to have been invited to the wedding but it was a simple affair on Zuckerberg's private jet.

When I asked to borrow twenty quid, he smiled and said, "Neither a borrower nor a lender be." He didn't buy a round.

My father said, "That's how he can afford those teeth."

Who did he take after? None of our relatives had received a CBE or won the Nobel Peace Prize, though a second cousin had once owned a betting shop.

While Colin-Cameron-Troy was in the toilet I said, "He thinks he's chocolate."

My brother said, "I think he's a twat."

My mother said, "I think I brought home the wrong baby."

My father said, "I need a smoke."

We voted three-to-one, to disinherit him. Turned the cold shoulder until he took the hint and went to join some other young entrepreneurs in the bistro across the street. Then we threw our coats over his chair, ordered another jug of punch, and never mentioned his name again.

~

Lynda Nash's Biography

Lynda lives across the Welsh border, and likes, in no particular order: cats, kids, countryside, peanut butter cups and poems that don't rhyme. Some of her un-rhyming poems have been published as a collection and some of her prose has found its way into books and magazines. She now spends her spare time stitching scraps of fabric into crafty creations and thinks the world needs more art and alliteration.

~

Lynda's Competition Judging Comments

It's an honour to be chosen as a judge, especially for a competition as esteemed as this one. The standard of writing made every story a pleasure to read, and whittling down the short list was no mean feat. Stories took me to unexpected places and unusual situations and introduced me to many unique characters – your writerly imaginations are amazing and I wanted you all to win. Congrats to the short list and kudos to the winner, whoever you may be.

WITCHES IN A DRAGON

Judge's story, by Christopher Fielden

1

"I hate dragons," said Mildred. "They're a pain in me nether regions."

Despite feeling annoyed with Mildred for causing their current predicament, Hilda was unable to fault her assessment of large reptiles. Being swallowed was bad enough, but the state of this thing's belly was beyond imagining. All sorts of items protruded from the stomach acid. Animal bones, a cart's wheel, a ship's mast—

"Is that a statue?"

"I think it is, Hild." Mildred was trying to wipe intestinal goo out of her hair, fighting a battle she was unlikely to win. There was more goo than hair. "Looks like the mayor's statue, the one that went missing from Chieftain's Hill last month." Mildred smirked. "Ain't he one of them dragon deniers?"

Hilda nodded. "How ironic."

"Well, at least this proves they exist, eh Hild?"

"Beyond doubt."

Hilda flicked the glowing tip of her wand around their fleshy prison. It was like a blood-filled cauldron; bubbling, brown and full of half-digested bits of Lord knows what. Hilda was knee deep in the intestinal quagmire and her irritation was rising.

"It took us weeks to brew that annihilation potion," Hilda said, clambering onto the statue's base. "Why didn't you use it?"

"Only in an emergency, you said, if there was nothing else we could do."

"I think the moments prior to our ingestion, particularly the final few seconds when the dragon drooled on us, could have been classed as an emergency." Hilda unlaced and removed one calf-length boot and poured fluid from it. Her stockings, which Mildred had knitted, were ruined.

"When you annihilate something, Hilda Jane Beauchamp, it's destroyed. Utterly obliterated. There ain't nothing left of it, save for dust. No head, no proof. And we're here for proof." A large blob of goo slid from the brim of Mildred's pointed hat onto her shoulder.

Hilda offered Mildred her hanky. A small one, embroidered with broomsticks.

"Oh, very funny, Hild." This was a hands-on-hips moment and Mildred didn't fail to take advantage of it.

All of her chins wobbled as she spoke. "Hilarious, that is. This is important."

Hilda sighed. Mildred was right. Dragons were posing a threat to humankind, but no one would do anything about it because there was little proof they existed. In the foothills of the mountains, where Hilda lived, farmers were losing crops, livestock and, more recently, farmworkers. This *was* important.

"I apologise, Mildred. The prospect of becoming dragon excrement isn't helping my mood or judgement."

Mildred's scowl dissipated and she looked around. "How are we going to get out of here?"

Hilda started rummaging through the pockets in her long, soggy dress. Then her shawl. Under her hat. In the folds of her cape.

"What you lookin' for?" Mildred asked.

"You'll see, if I can find it."

"You should use that bag I got you last solstice. Nice lookin'. Spacious. Lots of compartments so you can find stuff easy."

Hilda tutted. She didn't believe in bags. They always got in the way, especially when casting spells. And one might be liable to forget them; leave them in a tavern or at the alchemists. But pockets... pockets were different. They went everywhere with you and Hilda had a plethora of them. "It's in here somewhere..."

"What's in there somewhere?"

"Be patient, Mildred."

"Me feet's itchin', Hild. Might be me athlete's foot, but I think this stomach soup is starting to digest me toes. Hurry it up, will you?"

Hilda's fingers found what they were looking for. She pulled a small bayonet from a recess in her tunic and connected it to her wand.

Mildred looked at her, eyes so wide there was more white than iris. "Where'd you get *that*?"

"Old Mistress Birdwhistle gave it to me, years ago, when she first deemed me worthy of the title Sorceress."

"She never gave me one."

"Studying was not your forte, Mildred."

"I got the title of Sorceress though, didn't I?"

"Eventually..."

"And when I did, she gave me a hat."

"It's a nice hat."

Mildred glanced upwards. "Yeah, but it ain't no wand-bayonet, is it? I can't believe you've never shown it to me before."

"Shall we discuss this later, Mildred? I think we should probably focus on getting out of here."

"I s'pose we should. You going to use that fancy blade thing of yours – what I ain't got one of because I ain't clever enough – to cut us an exit?"

"Unless you have a better idea, yes."

"Ideas ain't my thing, Hild. I ain't very bright, remember?"

This could continue for days, Hilda thought. *If we live...* "Mildred, do you think a dragon's scales are as tough on the inside as they are on the outside?"

"Funny you should say that," Mildred replied, clambering out of the intestinal juices to stand on the statue's base, "cos I've worn dragon-scale armour."

Hilda raised an eyebrow. "When?"

"At a fancy dress party. I went as a knight. Borrowed it off that chevalier. You know, the one who was blessed when it came to fighting, but not so much in the face department. Had eyes like poached eggs, a nose like an overbaked baguette and a puckered mouth what looked like a cat's butthole. Bought a lot of love potions."

Hilda shuddered, wondering how many lives had been ruined by Mildred's elixirs.

"You know my love potions don't do nothing, right? They're placebos. All they do is make people more confident."

"You can read minds now?"

"No. I ain't that bright, remember? Your face says it all, Hild. Just got to observe. Anyway. As I remember it, the armour was very comfortable."

Hilda was about to ask whether comfort related to strength when a sudden bout of coughing made her stop. The air tasted of acid and her lungs hurt. She looked at Mildred; her chubby face shone with defiance, but her skin was blotchy and her eyes bloodshot. She looked exhausted. A dragon's gut is not a welcoming environment. They had to stop talking and escape.

"Thank you, Mildred, for your insight. I will be sure to take that into account."

Hilda used her wand to shine light around the dragon's stomach, while recalling anatomy classes from her training days. Organs, sinews, cartilage and all the other unpleasant things you find inside bodies are important to witchcraft, so Hilda had dissected many creatures. Of course, she'd never anatomised a dragon, but they were reputed – by those who acknowledged their existence – to share similarities with serpents and reptiles. Essentially, their digestive system was like that of a lizard, just bigger.

Hilda shone the light upwards, illuminating the round, muscular orifice they'd arrived through. "That must be the lower oesophageal sphincter."

"I thought sphincters were on the outside. Well, kind of. It's not like they see a lot of daylight between your ass cheeks, but—"

"There are multiple sphincters in the bodies of most creatures, Mildred, not just *that* one."

Mildred folded her arms. "Well, I'll consider myself educated."

Moving her wand slowly, Hilda followed the arc of the stomach lining to the back of the gooey pool the statue was standing in. "Beneath that, is the pyloric sphincter."

"Fascinating, that is. You're *so* clever. But, if I may ask... *so what*?"

"The dragon's midriff should be opposite. The belly is the softest external area and, therefore, the one we have the best chance of cutting through."

"I see." Mildred's scowl softened. She looked at the bayonet. "Do you think that little thing will cut through a dragon?"

"I don't know. But we have to try."

"Well, if anyone can save us, my money's on you." Mildred gave Hilda a hug. "And if it all goes tits up, there ain't no one else I'd rather die with."

Feeling tears welling, Hilda kissed Mildred's cheek, extracted herself from the embrace and jumped down from the statue. She steadied herself in the swamp of gastric detritus and raised her hand. The bayonet shone in the light emanating from the wand's tip.

"Do it, Hild. Gut the bugger."

Hilda lunged forward and swung the weapon. It tore through stomach lining. Their host lurched. Hilda managed to grab the statue's base, but Mildred lost her balance and fell from above her, disappearing with a splash. Hilda plunged her hand into the stomach juices, grabbed an arm and pulled. Mildred came to the surface, gasping.

"Are you alright?"

"Yeah," said Mildred. "He didn't like that much, did he?"

They looked at the wound Hilda had inflicted. The gash was long, but not deep enough.

Mildred spat, a glower on her face. "I got an idea, Hild. Give us a hand up onto the statue, will you?"

After some rather inelegant shoving, Mildred reached her desired destination and took a hip flask from her belt. She swigged and passed it down to Hilda, who took a sip. The elixir tasted medicinal – it soothed Hilda's throat and cleared her mind.

Mildred then pulled a stoppered vial of powder from her pocket, sprinkled it on her feet and undertook a short dance – the somatic elements of a spell.

Hilda marvelled at Mildred's dexterity. A voluminous woman working in a confined space should not be graceful, especially when clad in witches' attire that was both copious and sodden. But the precision of Mildred's footwork was pristine, her balance perfect. When the dance was complete, Mildred floated into the air and drew her wand. Crimson mist poured from her nose, masking her face in blood-shadow. From deep in her throat, the words of the magnify spell resonated. Hilda's wand, and bayonet, enlarged. The blade sparked with tendrils of fire and lightning.

Hilda felt her confidence grow. "Thank you, Mildred. Your witchcraft is impeccable."

Thrusting wand and bayonet forward, Hilda charged. She slashed upward, rending a gaping wound in the dragon's midriff. Fire and lightning sizzled. The stench of burnt flesh filled the air. Through the hole she'd made,

Hilda glimpsed the moon and stars.

Before she could celebrate, their host reeled. A tidal wave of stomach acid hit Hilda in the back, knocking her from her feet. She sank, swirling in a whirlpool of abdominal slime. *We've failed*, Hilda thought. *Two witches versus a dragon. What a stupid notion.* Her body was thrown violently back and forth. Something crashed against her head. Pain flashed, extinguished by blackness.

2

A slap stung Hilda's cheek. She opened her eyes and saw Mildred standing over her, a worried expression on her face.

"Sorry, Hild, did that harder than I meant to. Thought you was dead there for a moment."

Hilda sat up and rubbed the back of her head. "So did I. What happened?"

"You did it, Hild. Cut a hole so big in that thing's gut its stomach exploded outward. Took us with it."

Hilda looked around. They were on a mountain ledge, lit by moonlight. It was spattered with dragon debris. Scales stuck out of the rock face. Flesh and blood decorated everything. A stream of stomach juice was pouring away, over the side of the mountain. And they were in one piece, breathing, *alive*.

"That's one hell of a bayonet," said Mildred, a hint of jealousy in her voice.

Hilda nodded. "Especially when magnified by one of the most powerful witches who ever walked these mountains."

"Oh stop it, Hild, me head'll swell."

The bayonet was still enlarged, glimmering with

shreds of fire. "Well, I guess we can use it to cut off the dragon's—"

"Head?" The voice was deep and filled with loathing.

Hilda turned and saw a monstrous shape, looming in the shadows. It limped forward into the moonlight. The dragon was colossal, the carnage that was its midriff exuding a mass of entrails. Everything about it was black: its scales, its eyes, its wings, its claws – even its erupting innards. As it spoke, noxious smoke spiralled from its nostrils. "This time, I'll chew before I swallow."

It raised itself up onto its hind legs, spread its wings and bellowed, revealing a mass of granite-like teeth.

The beast lunged. A blast of rancid breath hit Hilda in the face, but failed to ignite, proving dragons need an intact digestive system to spew fire.

Claws slashed. Mildred darted left. Jaws snapped. Hilda ducked, but she wasn't fast enough. Her left arm erupted in pain. The dragon swung its head upwards, flinging her into the air.

As she reached the apex of her trajectory, Hilda experienced a moment of weightlessness. Looking down, she saw the dragon rise onto its hind legs and open its mouth. Its black throat glistened in the moonlight, like a doorway to the grave.

As she began to fall, Hilda saw Mildred point her wand. A bolt of energy hit the creature in the back. It roared, turning its head.

Hilda swung the wand-bayonet in a deadly arc. Fizzing through the air, spitting sparks of fire, it sliced through the dragon's exposed neck. As the monstrous head fell with a crash, the dragon's body slid off the mountain ledge, toppling out of sight.

Hilda landed heavily in a mound of intestines. Although disgusting, the guts were soft enough to break her fall. She lay still, fighting for breath. The dragon's head stared at her with lifeless eyes, wisps of vapour rising from dead nostrils.

Hilda felt Mildred take her hand and gently squeeze it. "You OK, Hild?"

There was an ugly gash on her left arm. Tentatively, Hilda moved her fingers. "I think so. Cut and bruised, not broken."

Mildred tore a strip of cloth from her dress and bandaged the wound. "That will have to do until we get home." She helped Hilda into a sitting position and they leant against a rock. With shaky hands, they took turns to drink from Mildred's flask.

After a few minutes of quiet, Hilda had regained some semblance of composure. She nodded at the dragon's head. "We have to make sure this is seen."

"We could put it on Chieftain's Hill, where the mayor's statue was. Replace a denier's likeness with what he's in denial of. Kind of poetic, eh?"

"More people will see it in the town square, especially if we take it there on market day."

"True." A sombre look clouded Mildred's face. "You think the deniers will say it's fake?"

"Probably."

"Don't see why they don't admit the problem exists. They must know. There's a food shortage because of ruined crops and disappearing cattle. It can't all be down to heatwaves and thieves. People are disappearing too."

"Politics, Mildred. There will be a reason. Money, relationships, power, control. Something like that."

"Or all of it." Mildred suddenly perked up. "Ooo, Hild, look." She got up, wandered over to the rock face covered in bits of dragon and bent down amidst the debris.

"What is it?"

"More proof." Mildred turned around. In her hands was an egg. It was the size of a watermelon and granite-black. "I guess he was a she."

"They'll have trouble denying the existence of dragons if that hatches. Come on, let's get the cart."

"I hope the horses haven't legged it."

"If they have, we'll find them."

As they hobbled towards the gully they'd used to hide the cart, Hilda removed the bayonet from her wand. It had returned to a normal size.

"It's a lovely bayonet, that is," said Mildred. "Wish I was clever enough to have one."

Hilda looked at the artefact in her hand. It marked a great achievement in her personal history, but Hilda was no fighter — today, she'd been lucky. Mildred was younger, more dextrous. It might be of more use to her.

"You're more than clever enough." Hilda proffered the bayonet. "Happy birthday."

"My birthday ain't for three months."

"Consider this an early gift."

Mildred gave Hilda a hug that hurt. It came from nowhere and crushed the air from her lungs. "You is the most special sister I ever had." Mildred released her and grinned. It was one of those grins that might last a week. Or more. "In return, you can have me hat."

Hilda looked at the misshapen thing on Mildred's head. "I couldn't possibly—"

"I insist."

They swapped items. Hilda removed her own hat and placed Mildred's on her head. It fitted perfectly, despite a noticeable disparity in their head sizes. Maybe it was more than just a hat.

Mildred attached the bayonet to her wand and swished it back and forth. "You know, seeing as how this ended up being a swapping of magical artefacts, this bayonet don't really count as a present. You'll have to get me another."

Hilda sighed. "Yes, Mildred."

3

After loading the dragon's head onto the cart – a process that took a lot of time, rope, horses and swearing – they took their seats and prepared to leave.

As the rising sun appeared to the east, Hilda looked down the mountainside and saw the dragon's body smashed on the rocks below. Out of its midriff, the mayor's statue protruded, surrounded by a giant ribcage. Stomach acid had eaten away at the more intricate parts of the statue, particularly the head, leaving it eyeless.

Hilda nudged Mildred and pointed. "An effigy to the futility of denial. Long may it remind us."

"What you on about, Hild? All I know is I'm gagging for a cuppa. And tea tastes better with cake. You got some cake in the larder, right?"

Hilda smiled. "Always."

"Good. I've had enough of this heroism malarkey. And I need a bath. That thing's innards are still playing havoc with me skin. Can we go home please?"

"Yes, Mildred, we certainly can."

Hilda flicked the whip above the horses' heads. The cart moved forward, and they began their journey home, with a cargo that might just change the future.

~

Christopher Fielden's Biography

Chris is a human being with a problematic brain. It's full of crazy ideas. Said ideas have no business associating with reality or becoming actual things. Unfortunately, sometimes they do. To Hull And Back is but one example. There are many others. Chris could have created a list at this point, but decided not to. You're welcome.

Fortunately for Chris, lots of other human beings suffer with similar defective brain issues and enter his competition. Entrants hope to take a trip on a motorcycle. To Hull. With a lunatic. They pay an entry fee and everything. Behavioural scientists are baffled.

Chris is considering starting a political party. Since writing the previous sentence, he's decided it would be too much work and has shelved the project. Instead, he'll be concentrating on writing his own stories until To Hull And Back reopens its doors in the summer of 2022.

'Witches in a Dragon' was first published by the British Fantasy Society in 2020. It was reprinted by WolfSinger Publications in *Crunchy with Ketchup* in 2021. A follow up story titled 'Baker's Zodiac', featuring more of Hilda and Mildred's antics, will be published by Comma Press in 2022.

Chris is a member of the ALCS, ASCAP, the British Fantasy Society, Clockhouse London Writers, the Mechanical Licensing Collective and Stokes Croft Writers.

You can learn more information than anyone could possibly want to know about Chris on his website:

www.christopherfielden.com/about/

~

Chris's Competition Judging Comments

This year, I received over 500 competition entries for the second time. The history of entry numbers looks like this:

- 2021: 524 (-58)
- 2019: 582 (+126)
- 2018: 456 (+97)
- 2017: 359 (+75)
- 2016: 284 (+68)
- 2015: 216 (+122)
- 2014: 94

This is the first time I've experienced a reduction in competition entry numbers. It had to happen at some point...

There could be any number of reasons for fewer entries, including the increased entry fee (although I've upped that every year to date and it hasn't made a difference), the pandemic, lots of lovely weather in the UK during July, the fact that the competition now runs biennially (every other year) instead of being open 24/7 (meaning it may drop off people's writing radars), a general dip in writing related online searches (my website traffic always dips during the UK's summer months, but it's more pronounced this year despite my site continuing to rank well for key search terms on Google and other search engines) etc.

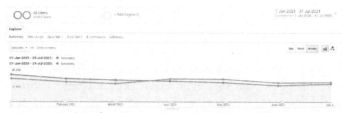

Screenshot from Google Analytics - sessions January to July 2021 vs 2020

The image above might be a bit small to see clearly, so here's the gist of what it means:

- The darker line (top on the left) shows sessions for 2021. The lighter line (bottom on the left) shows sessions for 2020.
- In January 2020, my website attracted 27,374 sessions (or visits) from 21,672 users (I get a lot of returning website visitors who use my website more than once a month). In January 2021 it attracted 32,086 visits from 25,488 users. January often results in the most monthly website visits of the year. I think this is because writers come back after the Christmas break with New Year resolutions to finish their book, write more etc. The year-on-year session figures for January show an increase of around 14.5%.
- In June 2020, my website attracted 22,700 visits from 17,979 users. In June 2021 it attracted 19,486 visits from 15,656 users. Website traffic often dips in June, but not as much as it did during 2021. The year-on-year figures for June show a decrease of around 14%.
- In July 2020, my website attracted 23,440 visits from 17,284 users. In July 2021 it attracted

21,453 visits from 18,442 users. This shows a decrease of around 8.5%.

As you may have deduced, I'm a stats geek. In the interest of not boring anyone that isn't, I'll leave it there and summarise by saying that visits were down in the summer months of 2021, even though To Hull And Back wasn't running in 2020. When the competition is open, I'd expect the number of sessions and visitors to increase. While my search engine rankings (the position my website appears in Google's search results when someone searches for something like 'short story competitions') do fluctuate, they have remained fairly consistent. This indicates that fewer people were searching for terms relating to writing competitions during the summer of 2021, which may be part of the reason for the drop in entry numbers. A lot of the world was in lockdown during the summer of 2020. Lockdown restrictions were being lifted in the spring / summer of 2021. That is likely to be a contributing factor in all of this.

Anyway, I decided to up the prize pot again next time the competition runs regardless. More on that shortly...

The early bird fee helped again this year, working better than previous years. At the end of April 2021, I'd received 238 entries, compared to 212 entries in 2019.

The flow of submissions during May and June were consistent with previous years (numbers up throughout). It was the tail end of June and most of July that were different. The 2019 figures were higher. On 20th July 2021, the overall number of submissions dropped behind those of 2019.

As usual, there were a large number of entries as the closing date approached: 230 in the final month, 133 in the final week and 58 on the final day. Last year, it was 312 in the final month, 162 in the final week, 56 on the final day. Writers love working to deadlines. I'm no exception.

I know I say this every year, but I'm NOT complaining about the amount of entries I receive – it's fantastic that so many people enter and support the competition. I'm extremely grateful and am confident that the number of entries will grow again in future. I simply share these stats because I find them interesting and it helps me find better ways of running To Hull And Back.

This year, I went to the Cambrian Mountains and Ceredigion in Wales to undertake the reading and judging. I started off in the mountains. There's no internet or phone signal up there and it's not a tourist hot spot. It's the perfect place to read.

One of my favourite writing and reading spots, above Llyn Brianne

I went to Llandovery and got a bit over-excited at the castle because it's guarded by a gurt big metal knight.

The Llandovery Knight, at Llandovery Castle

I went walking in the mountains to calm down.

Me, calmed down by fresh air and mountains

And then I headed to Mwnt in Ceredigion and did some more reading.

The mobile writing office parked up near Mwnt in Ceredigion, Wales

The weather was very changeable. It resulted in some spectacular rainbows.

Rainbow over Mwnt

I saw dolphins while walking along the cliffs. They weren't walking in the cliffs. I was. The dolphins were in the sea.

The cliffs of Ceredigion, Wales, UK

And then I stopped off in the mountains again on the way home, to do a bit more reading and procrastinating.

The mobile writing office back in the Cambrian Mountains

Are you suitable jealous? Good. That's enough photos.

The quality of the stories entered this year was awesome. There were lots of original ideas I hadn't seen before. Stories that are imaginative and unique resonate with me. They captivate my attention and inspire me.

Running To Hull And Back is a lot of work. The reading is always time consuming, even if the entries are fewer. Therefore, I've decided to make the following changes to how the competition runs next time around.

The opening and closing dates will be altered. Previously, the competition has always opened for submissions on 1st August and closed on 31st July. In future, it will open on 1st July and close on 30th June. The next competition will run in 2023. It will open for entries on 1st July 2022 and close 30th June 2023. The shortlist and winner announcements, and book publication date, will remain the same. This is to make the reading more manageable for me, give the other judges more time to evaluate the shortlist and the artist more time to incorporate the winner's head on the book cover. And it will give me more time to prepare the anthology for publication.

I will also be investigating alternative ways of advertising the competition. In 2021, I substantially increased my spend on social media ads. Most of that spend was concentrated on Facebook. I ran both video and static ads.

Here is an example of a static ad that I ran on Facebook during in July 2021.

PTO.

The engagement stats were good (wide reach, meaning lots of views, likes and shares) but the ads didn't result in many clicks to my website and, therefore, entries. Well... not in a way that could be tracked, anyway.

The increased spend resulted in some abusive comments and unfounded accusations of the competition being a scam.

Christopher Fielden so yet another scam

Like · **Reply** · Message · 4 w

I deleted anything abusive and replied politely to any false scam accusations, like the one above – an advantage of undertaking this detailed write-up every year is that it's easy for me to back up claims of legitimacy and transparency by simply sharing a link. My replies sometimes resulted in the person who had made the accusation removing their comment (meaning my replies, and any others, disappeared too). Sometimes, there was no response. Other times, the commenter either maintained their accusation or just said something non-committal. E.g. a reply from the same person below.

Christopher Fielden mm

Like · **Reply** · Message · 3 w

I'm pleased to say that other members of the writing community jumped to my defence in the comments. I'd like to say a special thank you to Debbi Voisey of Writers Supporting Writers for her kind help.

I also experienced a few complaints about the entry fee via advert comments. One chap said it was too expensive and used the V.S. Pritchett Short Story Prize as an example of why – they charge £7.50 for an entry, whereas I charge £15. I pointed out that I'm a one man band and don't have sponsorship, hence the fee, and that the V.S. Pritchett (which is a fantastic competition, by the way) has the Royal Society of Literature behind it. I also drew the chap's attention to the fact that my prize pot is over 3K and gives twenty cash prizes, whereas (from what I could see in the T&Cs) the VSP only gives one cash prize of 1K. My fee is double theirs, but my prize pot is triple. He said, 'Fair comment. Thanks anyway.'

Overall, the ads were time consuming to run and didn't work brilliantly. This means that I will move some of my ad spend away from social media next time round, and look at other online advertising and print advertising options.

In 2019, I concentrated on increasing the top six prizes. This time, I'm upping the lower fourteen prizes and adding twenty more for the long-listed writers. Therefore, for the 2023 contest, the prize pot will be increased as follows:

- Prize pot increased from £3,250 to £3,860:
  - First: £1,200
  - Second: £600
  - Third: £300
  - Three x highly commended: £150

- ○ Fourteen x shortlisted: £75 (up from £50 – £350 total increase to prize pot)
- ○ Twenty x longlisted: one x free early-bird entry to the next competition (with a value £13 each – £260 total increase to prize pot)
  - ▪ The cost of these twenty new prizes won't hit me until the 2025 contest runs, so it gives a bit of breathing space if entry numbers drop again in 2023

So there will be forty prizes in future.

In previous years, I've always upped the entry fee to help cover the increase in the prize pot. For 2023, I've decided to leave the entry fee the same as 2021. This is more risky for me, but I want to see if keeping the entry fee the same helps attract more entries. I'm highly likely to up the entry fee again in the future.

In 2019, I said I was going to investigate using Submittable to manage and automate the entry process. This would have removed a lot of admin work that I currently undertake manually. I found that, for my needs, the cost was over $2,000 a year and Submittable didn't do everything I required it to do. I also looked at other similar service providers. Some were a bit cheaper, but still too expensive. All of them had functional limitations, meaning none were ideal for my needs. To Hull And Back doesn't currently turnover enough money to make automation viable without reducing the prize pot and / or advertising spend. Therefore, I didn't pursue this further.

In 2019, I also said I'd consider working with other readers to help me decide the shortlist. The idea was to reduce my workload and incorporate different reading tastes during the selection process. I thought this might make the initial judging stages fairer. Relying on one person's (rather quirky) taste year after year can impact the diversity of the stories selected.

However, the first round of reading is very time consuming. So is the second. It usually takes me four or five rounds to finalise the shortlist. I decided that I couldn't ask anyone else to do the work for free. The amount of time it takes would have meant paying other people a lot of money, even if they worked for minimum wage. This would result in the competition making a substantial loss – something I can't afford to do. So, I decided to keep doing the shortlist selection myself for now. If the competition's turnover increases in the future, I will revisit this idea.

As always, I kept sponsorship in mind. So far, nothing has come to fruition.

This year, the competition is likely to make a small profit (the overall amount depends on anthology sales). The 2021 prizes are first £1,200, second £600, third £300, three x runner-up prizes of £150 and fourteen x shortlist prizes of £50 – total is £3,250. Other costs include PayPal charges, video production costs, admin costs, website maintenance costs, costs of publishing the anthology, advertising costs, the costs of putting on a book launch and, of course, the epic journey to Hull and back.

All the judges and everyone else involved with the competition continue to give their time for free, which I appreciate greatly. This is something I want to address in future... maybe next time, if the turnover allows.

As I've said before, the long-term aim is to provide a five-figure top prize to help the competition become more widely known and give humorous short stories a respected publishing platform to be celebrated from.

That is still my goal.

This year's anthology cover was designed by James Childs. I've known James most of my life. We became friends at school and play music together in rock bands Airbus and Little Villains.

Chris and James, modelling some new band merch while on tour in Belgium with Little Villains in 2019

The eBook version of the anthology was coded by Angela Googh this year. Ange codes the eBooks for a lot of the writing challenges I run. Having the eBook professionally coded means it looks better and is more accessible to readers who are visually impaired. I'd like to say a huge thank you to Ange for her meticulous hard work.

Entries this year came from a large number of locations around the planet. They include: Australia, Canada, Canary Islands, Croatia, France, Germany, Greece, India, Ireland, Israel, Italy, Malaysia, New Zealand, Northern Ireland, Portugal, Scotland, Singapore, South Africa, Spain, Sudan, Sweden,

Switzerland, Trinidad and Tobago, Ukraine, United Arab Emirates, USA and Wales.

I've kept track of different points of view used to tell the stories again this year (geekdom overload, but I loves it). Here are the figures:

- Stories written in the first person (I did, I said): 43%
- Stories written in the second person (you did, you said): 1%
- Stories written in the third person (she did, he said, they wanted): 51%
- Other (stories that were presented as a list, poem, album review, emails, journal / diary entries, letters, meeting minutes, phone calls, scientific papers, scripts, vignettes, or used both first and third person etc.): 5%

Compared to 2019, first person is down 4.5%, second person is unchanged, third person is up 1% and other is up 3.5%.

In 2019, 59 entries didn't obey the rules (just over 10% of 582 entries). In 2021, that figure decreased to 47 (just over 9% of 524 entries). Unfortunately, I had to disqualify 22 of these entries compared to 12 in 2019. Most of the disqualifications were either excessively over the word count limit, or failed to obey any of the rules.

If you weren't longlisted or shortlisted, please don't be disheartened. I receive a lot of entries and there are only twenty places on each list. I don't reject stories because I don't like them. I simply select the stories that are best suited to this competition.

That's it. The seventh To Hull And Back competition is complete. I've read hundreds of stories. I've laughed a lot. I've been surprised and delighted by some amazing writing. Thank you to everyone who has entered. This simply would not be possible without each and every one of you.

And as a final note, I'm pleased to say that To Hull And Back was recognised by Reedsy as one of the best writing contests of 2021. I must be doing something right :-)

Cheers me dears, Chris

A FINAL NOTE

Thank you to all the writers who entered the competition and everyone that purchases this anthology. Your continued support allows To Hull And Back to bring more attention to humorous writing.

While you wait for the next competition, why not take part in my writing challenges? They're all free to enter, every submission is published and money from book sales are donated to charity. Check them out here: www.christopherfielden.com/writing-challenges/

Until next time ☺

Chris Fielden

Printed in Great Britain
by Amazon